TROUBLE'S BREWING BEFORE
THE FOX HUNT!

Carole felt a terrible cringing sensation when she thought about what it was Stevie had done. Stevie's brothers would certainly try to get back at her. It would be one thing if they put up notes in the boys' room at school or if they short-sheeted her bed or replaced her lunch sandwich with dog food. It would be another thing altogether, however, if Stevie's brothers decided to aim their revenge at what Stevie loved best: horseback riding. There were all kinds of things they could do that could jeopardize Stevie's riding. The boys would know that and it would most certainly be their target. That was something Carole couldn't let happen.

It was time for The Saddle Club to come to the rescue, even if Stevie didn't know it. . . .

THE SADDLE CLUB

FOX HUNT

BONNIE BRYANT

A BANTAM SKYLARK BOOK®
NEW YORK • TORONTO • LONDON • SYDNEY • AUCKLAND

I would like to express my special thanks to Cynthia Zirkle and Kim Shinn for their help with this project.

—B.B.H.

RL 5, 009–012

FOX HUNT

A Bantam Skylark Book / June 1992

Skylark Books is a registered trademark of Bantam Books, a division of Bantam Doubleday Dell Publishing Group, Inc. Registered in U.S. Patent and Trademark Office and elsewhere.

"The Saddle Club" is a trademark of Bonnie Bryant Hiller. The Saddle Club design/logo, which consists of an inverted U-shaped design, a riding crop, and a riding hat is a trademark of Bantam Books.

ISBN 0-553-15990-9

Published simultaneously in the United States and Canada

Bantam Books are published by Bantam Books, a division of Bantam Doubleday Dell Publishing Group, Inc. Its trademark, consisting of the words "Bantam Books" and the portrayal of a rooster, is Registered in U.S. Patent and Trademark Office and in other countries. Marca Registrada. Bantam Books, 666 Fifth Avenue, New York, New York 10103.

PRINTED IN THE UNITED STATES OF AMERICA

CWO   0 9 8 7 6 5 4 3 2 1

STEVIE LAKE PASTED a smile on her face. It wasn't easy to do under the circumstances. There she was at the dinner table, surrounded by her three brothers. They were giving her a hard time. Normally she would have given back equally, but tonight was different. Tonight her boyfriend, Phil Marston, was a dinner guest. Stevie didn't like it when Phil saw her nastier side, though it was quite a temptation considering the ribbing the two of them were getting.

Chad, her eldest brother, had started it all.

"So, tell me, Stevie," he'd said. "Just where are you and Phil going tonight after dinner?"

"We're going to an organizing meeting for the mock hunt," she'd said evenly.

"Oh, you hunt mocks?" her twin brother, Alex, had

I

asked. "They've certainly been a menace to the local farmers."

"Alex!" Stevie had said between her teeth.

Phil had just smiled. "Not exactly, Alex," he'd said patiently, acting as if he thought Alex really didn't know what it meant. "It's mock—as in pretend. It's a pretend fox hunt being sponsored by Stevie's Pony Club. It's to prepare all of us for the real fox hunt that is taking place at my Pony Club."

"Oh, right," Chad had piped in. "That's when everybody dresses up in red jackets and chases after foxes while yelling unintelligible things and drinking brandy from flasks, right?"

"Tallyho!" her youngest brother, Michael, contributed.

Now Stevie was fuming. There were many times in her life when she'd wished she were an only child. This was one of those times. She imagined what it would be like to have a calm, intelligent discussion of fox hunting with her parents and Phil.

"I mean, is fox meat really all that good?" Alex asked.

"Aw come on," Chad said to him. "Haven't you ever heard the famous description of fox hunting by Oscar Wilde, the English playwright?" Chad was in ninth grade and enjoyed showing off his superior knowledge to everybody else in the family. Alex and Michael waited for him to continue. "He called it 'the un-speakable in pursuit of the inedible.'"

Michael and Alex howled with laughter.

Stevie grimaced. "Shows how much you know," she said. "Fox hunting is an old and honorable sport. In England, where there are a lot of foxes, they're viewed as a pest and the farmers often really do want them to be caught as long as it's humane. Here in America, where there are just a few foxes, they are rarely caught and even more rarely killed. In fact, most hunters would be disappointed if the hounds were to catch the fox. See, we want that same fox to be available to lead us on a merry chase the next time we go fox hunting." The instant the phrase "merry chase" left her lips, she was sorry.

"A merry chase!" Chad howled. Alex and Michael joined in. Even Stevie's parents seemed to be having trouble keeping their faces straight. Stevie blushed, and that made her all the angrier.

It just wasn't easy living with three brothers. That was one reason why Stevie loved horseback riding so much. She was the only one in her family who rode horses. It was a place she could be alone—or at least without her obnoxious brothers. Of course, she wasn't completely alone on horseback. When she went riding at her nearby stable, Pine Hollow, she was usually with her best friends, Carole Hanson and Lisa Atwood, and sometimes she was with Phil. This time, on the mock hunt and the real fox hunt, she was going to be with all of them, and she couldn't wait.

Stevie, Lisa, and Carole were three very different girls, but they had one big thing in common: horses. In fact, they loved horses and riding so much that they had formed a club. They called it The Saddle Club. Members had to be horse crazy and they had to be willing to help one another out of all kinds of jams. Phil, who lived a few towns away and belonged to a different Pony Club, was an out-of-town member of The Saddle Club. There were a few other riders they'd met who were out-of-town members, too. There were no other riders who were horse crazy enough in Willow Creek, Virginia, where the girls lived, but that was fine with Stevie, Lisa, and Carole. The three of them had plenty of fun on their own.

"Actually, there's a lot of misinformation around about fox hunting," Phil said, once the laughter had quieted down. "We've been doing a lot of reading on the subject at Cross County—that's my Pony Club— and one thing I thought was interesting was that only the huntsman, the Master of the Hounds, and the whippers-in are doing any actual hunting. The rest of us are just along for the ride."

"You mean you're not armed?" Chad asked sarcastically.

"Nobody on a fox hunt is armed," Stevie said, regaining her composure. "See, it's just a really good excuse for a cross-country ride with your friends over fences and through fields."

"Right," Phil added. "The exciting part is that you never know where the hunt is going to go. It's not like going on a trail ride."

Stevie couldn't believe how polite Phil was being to her brothers. It was much more than they deserved.

"It sounds very exciting to me," Alex said. He turned to his father. "I don't know that we should allow Stevie to go on this thing. She's so excitable. . . ."

"Ahem," Mrs. Lake said. That was a subtle signal that Alex was pushing the boundaries. The subtlety was lost on Michael. He plowed right on ahead, turning to Alex.

"But didn't you say that the only reason Stevie wanted to do this thing was because Phil was doing it?"

After the angry flash of red cleared through Stevie's head, she kept herself from leaping for her little brother's throat by imagining how much fun it would be to torture him to death. Nothing fast, just slow and really painful—in full view of all of his stuffed animals. And then, for Chad and Alex—

"Ahem!" Mr. Lake said. "I think it's time to change the subject. In fact, if we don't change the subject, I think I may disinvite some of my family members to the circus, which is coming to town in two weeks." The subtlety of that remark was not lost on anybody.

There was a traveling circus that did a few days of shows in all the nearby towns every year, and it was a particular favorite of the Lake family. Stevie's brothers were silenced quickly.

"Oh, right, the Emerson Circus," Phil said. "It's coming to Cross County soon, too. It's a great circus. My favorite part is always the clowns."

"Not me. I like the trained animals," Stevie said. "Especially the horses."

"Anyone for dessert?" Mrs. Lake asked brightly.

"I'll help clear," Stevie said.

"My, she's being domestic!" Chad teased. "Looks like she wants to show off for somebody. I wonder who?"

When Stevie was pretty sure Phil couldn't see, she gave Chad her nastiest look. "I'm just going to help Mom because it's your night to do it, and last time you cleared, you broke a glass. Remember?"

Before he could answer, she was at the sink and had the water turned on. That made enough noise so that she could grumble and nobody could hear her. At least Phil couldn't hear her.

The rest of dinner was relatively uneventful, primarily because Chad got three phone calls from girls in his class and spent most of dessert promising to call them back later. He gobbled down his pudding, then dashed for the phone to make good on his promises.

Stevie sighed with relief. He was always the ring leader of her brothers. As long as he wasn't around, things might be a little bit quiet.

After she and Phil cleared the table, Mrs. Lake excused them and told them to be on their way to Pine Hollow. After all, she didn't want the two of them to be late for the meeting.

Stevie couldn't get out of the door fast enough.

It was a cool evening. Pine Hollow was a ten-minute walk from Stevie's house, and both of them were glad nobody had offered to drive them over. They would get to be alone for a few minutes.

"I'm sorry about that—" Stevie began, slipping her hand into Phil's.

He squeezed her hand affectionately. "Always remember, Stevie, I've got sisters where you've got brothers. Sisters can be just as mean and vindictive as brothers. Chad, Alex, and Michael don't bother me at all."

"Well, they bother me a lot and you can bet I'm going to get even with them for that! I mean the teasing is one thing and is usually fair, but they were being downright rude. Imagine making such fun of fox hunting!"

"A lot of people do," Phil reminded her. "A lot of people think it's an odd sport."

"Then they just don't understand it, do they?"

7

"Nope, they don't understand it at all," Phil agreed.

"So I suppose we just better keep it a secret to ourselves, right?"

He winked at her. "Sure thing," he said. "Only it's going to be hard when we're riding across people's fields and backyards in hot pursuit of a fox, isn't it?"

"We'll do it on tiptoe," Stevie suggested. "They'll never know we're there."

Phil laughed. Stevie liked it better when the two of them laughed about fox hunting together than when other people, like her brothers, were laughing at them.

It was exciting to see the crowd in Max Regnery's office. Max and his mother, Mrs. Reg, ran Pine Hollow and the Pony Club, Horse Wise. It seemed that all of Horse Wise was there, but all of Cross County was there, too, along with Phil's instructor, Mr. Baker. Stevie and Phil waved to Carole and Lisa and grabbed spots near them on the floor. Everybody was jammed and crammed into Max's office. Nobody wanted to miss a word.

Mr. Baker spoke first. He explained that the two main purposes of a mock hunt were to have fun and to learn about hunting. Riders would be assigned jobs. One would be the fox, another rider would be the Master of the Hounds, one would be the huntsman, several would be whippers-in, quite a few would be hounds. The rest would be what he called "the field." Then Mr. Baker took a few minutes to explain what the Master, the huntsman, and the whippers-in were supposed to do. Stevie listened intently as the instructor told them that in a real hunt, the person who was totally in charge of everything except the actual tracking of the fox was the Master. The huntsman was in charge of tracking. The whippers-in were there to help the huntsman and help keep the hounds on the track. The best way to learn about how the real hunt was going to work was to have the mock hunt be as real as possible.

"And now Max has a few words for you," Mr. Baker said, turning the meeting over to Max.

Max explained to the riders that they were expected to be at Pine Hollow by seven-thirty on Saturday morning, that the hunt would take place beginning at eight-thirty and they would need every minute of that hour for tacking up and final organizing. He went over the dress requirements and the equipment everybody should have with them. He also explained that he and Mr. Baker would assign the roles of hounds for the hunt. "We'll appoint a Master, and that job will go to the person who has shown the most work on learning about fox hunts. We'll also choose a huntsman, a few of the whippers-in, and someone devious to be the fox," he said.

Max continued. "Now, there's one final thing I can't say too often, so I'm going to say it now, and I'm going to say it again and again until I'm sure all of you know it. A fox hunt—even a mock one—is something we can do only with the permission of the landowners around Pine Hollow and Cross County. Mr. Baker and I have spent some time making arrangements with the farmers around Pine Hollow and his stable so that our hunts aren't confined to our own land. We will be riding on other people's property with their specific permission, and we must never forget that we are their guests. We will ride only where we are permitted, when we are permitted. We will leave all gates exactly as we found them; we will leave the land exactly as we found it. Anyone who violates these rules of conduct, who goes on land where we are not welcome, who leaves gates open or trash behind, will be dismissed from these hunts immediately. There will be no exceptions. Am I making myself clear?"

All around the room, the young riders nodded. One of the first things young riders had to learn was where they could ride and where they couldn't. If a farmer or landowner permitted riding on his or her property, it was always essential to be a courteous and considerate guest.

"Any questions?" Max asked.

Veronica diAngelo raised her hand. Stevie grimaced, wondering what she was going to say. Veronica was just about her least-favorite person at Pine Hollow. She was a rich girl who was very selfish and much more concerned with how she was dressed than how she was riding.

"Yes, Veronica?"

"Isn't there traditionally a party after a hunt?" she asked. It was typical of Veronica to be thinking about a party instead of about the hunt.

"I was just getting to that," Max said. "Horse Wise will be hosting a hunt breakfast following the mock hunt on Saturday. We'll have our organizing meeting for that on Tuesday after riding class. Please plan to be here. That's all for now. I'll see my riders on Tuesday, and we'll welcome everybody back here on Saturday for the mock hunt. Until then, well, tallyho!"

Just hearing the word, silly as it sounded, made Stevie feel the excitement of the upcoming hunt. She was thrilled by the idea of the chase—the ultimate game of hide-and-seek—riding wildly across the rolling Virginia countryside, under branches, over streams and obstacles, free of paths, accompanied by friends. It was going to be wonderful and exciting, and she could hardly wait.

First, however, there was something else she had to take care of. When she'd said good night to Phil, Lisa, and Carole, she set her mind to her next task: revenge.

STEVIE HARDLY SLEPT a wink that night or the next. Her mind was so filled with wonderful ideas of things to do to her brothers that she simply didn't have time for sleep. By the time Monday morning came, her plan was complete. Her goal was to humiliate her brothers totally without letting them know—for sure—who was responsible. The only way to do that was to do it where they would never find out. For that, Stevie chose the girls' room at her school.

Stevie and her brothers all went to a private school in Willow Creek called Fenton Hall. A lot of the girls who rode at Pine Hollow also went to Fenton Hall, including Veronica diAngelo, a fact Stevie preferred to ignore most of the time. That Monday morning as she walked to school, putting the finishing touches on her plot, she particularly tried to ignore it. It wasn't easy, though, since Veronica was walking right next to her, talking a mile a minute about something Stevie was sure she didn't care the slightest bit about.

"All the best people do it, you know," Veronica said. "I mean, I've been trying to convince Max to do this for years."

"What are you talking about?" Stevie asked.

"Why, the fox hunt, of course. I mean, it's been a tradition among the finest families in Virginia since colonial days. . . ." Veronica let the thought hang.

Stevie groaned inwardly. Veronica was actually a pretty good rider, but her interest in riding ran much more toward what "the finest families" did than toward the hard work and fun involved. She cared more that her outfit matched the saddle pad worn by her pure-bred Arabian mare, Garnet, than she did that Garnet was comfortable with the bit she'd chosen for her. She cared a lot more about her horse's pedigree, which was considerable, than she did about her own perform-ance. As Stevie considered these facts about Veronica, she once again concluded that she really despised Ve-ronica.

"Finest families?" Stevie echoed innocently. "Well, I guess that lets you out. After all, you just come from a tiny little family with one spoiled daughter. In my fam-ily, we've got four fine children. That's got to make us a fine family, doesn't it?"

Veronica gave her a withering look and then began walking faster to catch up to a group of girls walking ahead of Stevie. Stevie sighed with relief. Veronica was a complete pain, and every time Stevie could put her in her place, she was pleased. Today, she thought, was going to be a wonderful day in spite of the fact that she hadn't quite completed the reading assignment for English and absolutely didn't understand the word problems her math teacher had assigned over the weekend, so they weren't done at all. She'd find a way around those trivial issues because anyone who was as good at revenge as Stevie was could surely talk two teachers out of detention!

It turned out that Stevie's English teacher was sick. In an instant, all of her problems were solved. Instead of English, she had a study hall. In the first place, that gave her an extra day to finish the reading assignment—plus the additional reading that was assigned. It also gave her time to look over the word problems, which, when she actually *looked* at them, didn't seem so tough. Finally, it gave her time to put the finishing touches on a few little signs and then make an extended visit to the girls' room.

"I'm feeling a little funny in my stomach," she said to the study-hall monitor.

"Do you want to go to the nurse's office?"

"No, just to the girls' room. Okay?"

"Should I come with you?" the nice woman asked.

That, of course, was the last thing Stevie needed or wanted. "No, no, I'll be fine. I may just be a little while. . . ."

The woman smiled. "Take your time," she said.

That, of course, was the first thing Stevie needed and wanted. She practically flew out of the study hall.

From her backpack, she brought out the signs she'd typed neatly on her mother's computer the night before, when she told her mother she was working on her English assignment.

ATTENTION ALL NINTH-GRADE GIRLS

Chad Lake has a new girlfriend. Her name is Valerie Ann Jones and she goes to Willow Creek High School. His previous girlfriend, as many of you know, was Virginia Ames. He carved Virginia's initials on his lacrosse stick. He's now added a "J" to that and has told Valerie that he *just* put her initials on his stick. Doesn't she deserve to know the truth? Call her at 555-3992 and tell her!

Stevie had used some of her study-hall time to draw a picture of Chad's lacrosse stick, before and after, at the bottom of the page. She thought she'd done a pretty good job of it. She took some tape out of her backpack and posted it high on the mirror where everybody would see it. She was pretty confident it would stay there all day long. The teachers all used a different girls' room; her note wouldn't be discovered until the cleaning people got there at night.

Next, it was Alex's turn. That was easier, though there was a good chance one of the girls would tear the note down. It informed anybody who cared to read it that Alexander Lake was undecided which one of his classmates—Stevie's classmates, too—he liked best, Andrea or Martha. He was currently leaning toward Andrea, but Martha *might* be asked to the upcoming middle-school dance because Alex had been talking about how great she'd looked doing jump shots in basketball the other day. Stevie was especially proud of the part about the jump shots. It was absolutely true, too. Alex hadn't been able to stop talking about it at dinner on Friday.

Finally, Stevie had a note for all the fourth-grade girls. It told anybody who cared to read it that her little brother, Michael, wore Spiderman underwear.

Just as she was zipping the pocket on her backpack and preparing to return to the study hall and her math word problems, the girls'-room door opened, and in walked her least favorite classmate, Veronica diAngelo.

"Well, hello," Veronica said sweetly and insincerely. Stevie grunted in response. Part of Stevie wanted to flee from the girls' room. Another part of her really wanted to know how Veronica would react to her anti-brother plot. She hesitated for a second, weighing the benefits, and then decided to wait. She turned on the water and washed her hands, very carefully.

Veronica read every word of all three of Stevie's notes. She couldn't contain her surprise. When she was done, she looked at Stevie, who was by then meticulously drying her hands with a paper towel.

"Girlfriends' initials carved into a hockey stick? Spiderman underwear? Is this what you meant by describing yours as a fine family?" Veronica smirked. Then, without waiting for a response, because none was possible, she brushed past Stevie and out into the hall.

Stevie fumed. It was one thing for her to dump on her brothers and make fun of them and try to wreak revenge on them. It was another thing, entirely, when Veronica diAngelo did it. Stevie would get even with her, too.

Four girls were going into the bathroom as Stevie left it. It gave her great pleasure to hear gasps and giggles from the foursome a few seconds later. Her scheme was working already.

But first, it was time for word problems.

"NICE GOING, STEVIE," Polly Giacomin said, clapping her on the back before the Horse Wise meeting came to order.

"That's the third one," Carole said to Lisa, observing Polly. "What on earth is going on?"

Lisa shook her head. "I don't know," she said, "but when so many people are congratulating Stevie, it gives me the willies. It's got to mean big trouble."

"My sentiments exactly," Carole said. "I think we'd better look into this."

"Look into what?" Stevie asked, overhearing the tail end of the conversation.

"Look into why everybody is clapping you on the back and congratulating you," Lisa said. "What have you done now?"

"Oh, it's just a touch of revenge," Stevie said. "Another ingenious plot by the famous, or should I say *in*famous, Stevie Lake."

"*Big* trouble," Lisa said to Carole, who nodded agreement.

"Well, it has to do with my troublesome brothers," Stevie began. "See, when Phil came for dinner on Saturday, they were total pains, teasing Phil and me and making fun of fox hunting. I couldn't let them get away with that, could I? I just *had* to take steps."

"Steps, maybe," Carole assented. "Leaps, definitely not. What did you do?"

Stevie reached into her pocket and brought out a copy of each of the signs she'd hung up in the girls' rooms at school. She handed them to Carole. Lisa read them over Carole's shoulder. She couldn't contain her gasp of horror.

"Aren't I wonderful?" Stevie asked proudly. "I think I'll go into the Revenge Hall of Fame."

"If you live that long," Carole said.

"And if somebody doesn't institutionalize you before then," Lisa added. "Are you totally out of your mind?"

"What do you mean?" Stevie asked, suddenly realizing that her best friends didn't share her enthusiasm for her prank.

Lisa and Carole looked at one another. The look was silent, but it said worlds. It said that they couldn't believe how naive their wonderful friend Stevie could be. Sometimes she got so caught up in her schemes that she completely forgot to look at the effect they were going to have on other people and what might happen in retaliation.

"You tell her," Carole said. That was probably a good decision. Lisa tended to be more diplomatic than Carole.

"We mean you're crazy!" Lisa said, very undiplomatically.

"And what's wrong with that?" Stevie demanded.

"Everything," Carole said. "Look, a little teasing is one thing, but what you've done to your brothers is public humiliation. They aren't going to let you get away with that!"

"And there are *three* of them," Lisa added.

"Oh, come off it," Stevie said, shrugging off her friends' concerns. "You two just don't know how it goes between me and my brothers."

"Oh, yes, we do," Carole said. "And it starts with a *T,* and that stands for Trouble. You haven't heard the last of this."

"It's no big deal," Stevie said.

"If that's the case, why is it that everybody keeps clapping you on the back?" Lisa asked.

Carole felt a terrible cringing sensation when she thought about what it was Stevie had done. Stevie's brothers would certainly try to get back at her. It would be one thing if they put up notes in the boys' room at school or if they short-sheeted her bed or replaced her lunch sandwich with dog food. It would be another thing if they tried to sabotage her friendship with Phil, though Carole suspected that Phil would know what was really going on. It would be another thing altogether, however, if Stevie's brothers decided to aim their revenge at what Stevie loved best: horseback riding. There were all kinds of things they could do that could jeopardize Stevie's riding. The boys would know that and it would most certainly be their target. That was something Carole couldn't let happen.

It was time for The Saddle Club to come to the rescue, even if Stevie didn't know it.

"We've got to talk," Carole whispered into Lisa's ear.

"I was just thinking the same thing," Lisa whispered back.

"What are you two whispering about?" Stevie asked.

"Nothing," they said together.

Stevie was about to insist that they tell her when Max saved the day.

"Horse Wise, come to order!" he commanded. The room was completely silent.

LISA USUALLY ENJOYED every minute of the Horse Wise meetings—even a business one like this, when most of what was discussed was who was going to bring what for the "hunt breakfast" on Saturday after the mock hunt. This time, however, all she could think of was the disaster that Stevie was courting with the pranks aimed at her brothers. The Saddle Club was going to have to come to Stevie's rescue—even though Stevie was refusing to acknowledge she was even in trouble.

It took some maneuvering, some fast writing, and some lightning reflexes to deliver notes to Stevie and Carole during the Horse Wise meeting, but by the time scraps of paper had flown back and forth quickly several times, it was all set up. Lisa had managed to get

Stevie to invite her and Carole to Stevie's house after Horse Wise for an emergency Saddle Club meeting. It was going to mean a late start for her homework that night, but some things were simply more important than homework.

The three girls walked back to Stevie's house together, chatting about the mock hunt as they went. Max had talked more about what was going to happen, and they had planned the breakfast.

"Wasn't Veronica hysterical?" Stevie asked. "Imagine—she wanted us to have champagne!"

"I liked the bright red color her face turned when you suggested that ginger ale would do the trick," Carole said.

"Especially when I told her it was what all the finest families drank," Stevie concluded, smirking proudly. Then she explained about the conversation she'd had with Veronica about the "finest families." Lisa thought it was just like Veronica to be concerned about that.

"You know, Veronica is such a pain that I wish there were a way to keep her out of the fox hunt at Cross County," Stevie said.

"Watch out," Lisa said to Carole, still looking at Stevie. "She's got that gleam in her eye, and you know that means trouble."

"Don't worry," Stevie assured her friends. "The only

trouble I have in mind is trouble for Veronica. Nothing will go wrong with us and our fun at both the mock hunt and the real one. That's a promise."

Lisa hoped very much that that was a promise Stevie would be able to keep, and she intended to see that it was.

The Lakes were all home when the girls arrived. It took them only about two and a half minutes to swoop through the kitchen and get everything they needed for their Saddle Club meeting so they didn't actually see anyone, but Lisa and Carole both called greetings into the den, where Stevie's parents were watching television.

"Where are your brothers?" Carole asked, slipping an apple into one pocket and a package of graham crackers into another. She held a soda can under one arm and carried an assortment of cheeses on a plate.

"Who knows? Who cares?" Stevie said airily. "Chad's probably listening to the awful music he likes, unless, of course, his ear is tired from all the phone calls he's had from his girlfriend yelling at him." She giggled.

Even though Lisa and Carole thought that what Stevie had done was more than unkind and very dangerous, they had to admit it was pretty funny. The idea of Chad's thinking his girlfriend wouldn't find out about his previous girlfriend, and about the curious similarity of their initials, was pretty silly. Chad sort of deserved some kind of comeuppance about that.

"Alex, on the other hand," Stevie went on confidently, "has probably decided he doesn't like either Martha or Andrea. My guess is that the next girl he's going to get a crush on is Amy. He was talking about her today—something about the interesting report she'd given to the class about Phoenicians. Imagine that, being interested in Phoenicians! He's very fickle, you know."

Lisa picked up the grapes and the marshmallows. "Let's go," she said, heading for the stairs. She was quite convinced that all three of Stevie's brothers would be standing at the top of the stairs, ready to murder Stevie and anybody who happened to be with her on her way to her room. She realized that the marshmallows and grapes wouldn't give her much protection, but they could be thrown and might possibly serve to confuse the enemy, if not to dominate them. She plucked a couple of grapes and held them in her right hand as they mounted the stairs.

"With Michael, of course, it's a different thing," Stevie said, leading the way upward. "The only way anybody will know if he really *does* wear Spiderman underwear is if they see them, and I don't think any of the girls will—unless, of course, he wears his white shorts. But he's already nervous about the issue. This morning he told Mom that he had an awful headache and couldn't go to school. Just wait till he goes back tomorrow and has to face the girls in his class—he'll get a taste of his own medicine then. I can't wait."

Lisa grimaced and followed Stevie up the stairs. Her friend was definitely playing with fire, and she was being more than a little mean. It wasn't her best side.

The boys' rooms were all closed tightly. The sound of heavy metal blared from Chad's room as Stevie had predicted. Bleeps of an electronic game came from the room Alex and Michael were sharing.

Stevie looked at her friends and shrugged. "See? I told you. Nothing's happening. The three of them just know that they got what they deserved. There's no trouble brewing here. Trust me."

Lisa and Carole looked at one another. They hoped that Stevie was right. For now, anyway, nothing seemed to be going on that required The Saddle Club to come to Stevie's rescue. That meant that Lisa and Carole could relax a little bit and simply enjoy their second-favorite activity—talking about horses.

"How are you and Comanche doing?" Stevie asked Lisa.

Lisa had ridden a horse named Pepper almost exclusively since she'd started riding and had only recently switched to Comanche when Pepper retired. Lisa missed Pepper and his sweet disposition. Comanche was turning out to be a handful for her.

"Only so-so," she said. "The last time I rode him, I spent an awful lot of time trying to get him to do what I wanted him to do instead of what *he* wanted to do."

"He's very headstrong," Carole agreed. "I always thought that was why he and Stevie got along so well," she added pointedly.

Stevie laughed. "We were a pair, weren't we? But now that I'm riding Topside, I realize that Comanche could be difficult."

"It may be that Comanche really isn't a good horse for you," Carole said. "You know, it's really important that a rider and a horse be matched carefully. Horses have personalities—"

"—just like people," Lisa finished for her. It was a familiar idea and one that she knew was very true. "See, I figured that since I like Stevie so much, I'd like a horse with a personality like hers," Lisa went on. "What I found, however, was that *liking* Stevie and trying to tell her what to do are two different things."

Lisa was afraid she might have hurt Stevie's feelings, but then Carole laughed, and after that Stevie laughed even harder than Carole, so Lisa knew that what she'd said was okay. She laughed, too. It felt very good to laugh after doing almost nothing but worrying ever since she'd learned about Stevie's not-so-practical jokes.

"You might talk to Max about trying another horse,

then," Carole suggested. "He knows it's no fun to spend your whole time arguing with your horse."

"But shouldn't I be learning something from it?" Lisa asked.

Carole scratched her chin. This was a good question about horses, and Carole liked to think about good questions before answering them. "You're always supposed to learn from riding," she began. "But you're also supposed to have fun. When learning means blisters on your hands from tugging at reins and sore muscles from kicking a horse, something's wrong, and it's no better for the horse than it is for you. You're a good rider, Lisa, for a relative beginner, but you're not as good as you're going to be one day. When that day comes, Comanche will be no trouble for you. In the meantime, you can learn plenty from a horse who isn't so much trouble. Why don't you ask Max about riding Diablo? He was some trouble when he first came to Pine Hollow, but Max has been doing a lot of work with him, and he seems gentle as can be now."

"You think he'd let me ride Diablo?"

"Don't know why not," Carole said.

"Oh, he's a sweetie," Stevie said. "And I remember Max saying that he used to belong to someone who did a lot of hunting with him. I bet he'll be great in the field. It's important to have a horse with experience— one who won't bolt off when he hears the hounds barking and baying. Say, what *is* baying, anyway?"

"Oh, it's sort of a howling sound hounds make," Carole said. "But what we want to hear from them is 'full cry.'"

"Is that one of those terms?" Lisa asked. Carole nodded. She had obviously been studying the list that Max had given all the members of Horse Wise, which was a sheet of fox-hunting terms. He'd just said that they were expected to be familiar with them. A lot of them seemed odd, and some were downright silly.

"My favorite thing from the list was 'couple,'" Lisa said.

"Like Phil and me?" Stevie asked. She obviously had *not* been studying the list.

"Not unless you and Phil are dogs," Lisa teased.

"Hounds," Carole corrected her. "They are always called hounds, never dogs, unless you mean only a male. And a couple is a pair of hounds. They are counted in couples because they are trained in couples and often work in couples. So, if our fox hunt has forty-five hounds in the pack, we call that twenty-two and a half couples."

"Strange," Stevie remarked.

"Tradition," Carole explained. "Fox hunting has more traditions than Pine Hollow." She tugged her list of terms out of her jeans pocket and glanced at it. "Here's another one," she said. "Capping fee."

"Oh, I know that," Lisa said. "It's what the riders pay to go along on the hunt. Originally, back in the old days, the hunt secretary would collect silver from the riders in his riding cap, and that's where the name comes from."

"Let me look at this list," Stevie said, borrowing the paper from Carole. She studied the words. "Here's one. 'Holloa.'" She pronounced it as if it rhymed with the Hawaiian greeting, "aloha."

"No, that's pronounced 'holler.'" Carole said.

"All right, then, what does it mean?"

"Holler," Lisa explained.

"It's the call a whipper-in makes when he spots the fox breaking cover."

"And breaking cover means running out into the open," Lisa told Stevie.

"I didn't realize how much information there was on that list," Stevie said a little sheepishly. "I guess I've got some work to do for the fox hunt, and I guess it's not going to be done in the girls' room at Fenton Hall."

Lisa felt some relief, and the look on Carole's face said that she shared the feeling. As long as Stevie spent time concentrating on the list Max had given the riders, she wouldn't have time to put up any more notices in the girls' room at Fenton Hall. That might not get her out of the hot water she was already in, but it would keep her from getting into any more. For now, that was as much as The Saddle Club could hope for.

There was the sound of a car horn outside Stevie's

house. That meant that Carole's father was there to pick her up. The Saddle Club meeting was over. Lisa and Carole piled up the wrappers and cans from their snack, loaded them all onto a plate, and took everything down to the kitchen, calling farewells to Stevie as they went. Stevie barely acknowledged them, though. She was too intent studying her list of hunting terms.

4

IN SPITE OF everything Stevie had said to Carole and Lisa, she *was* nervous. Since everybody at Fenton Hall, to say nothing of everybody in all of Willow Creek, seemed to know exactly what she had done to her brothers, it seemed a certainty that it had come to their attention. Still, there was no reaction from them.

Stevie stood in front of the mirror in her room, giving her hair a final comb, and asked herself the Sixty-Four-Dollar Question: *When?* Then there was the Sixty-Four-Thousand-Dollar Question: *What?* The mirror didn't answer her. Was it possible, she wondered, just barely possible, that they wouldn't retaliate in some form? Would they let her get away with her mean notes based on the idea that those notes were just desserts for the teasing she and Phil had suffered?

The mirror didn't have to answer that question. Stevie could do it all by herself. The answer was: *no way.*

Stevie slipped into her jacket, picked up her backpack, and headed downstairs and out the door. As usual, she was late. Her brothers had all left for school, so she didn't have to worry about retaliation on her way. All she had to worry about was the fact that they would have gotten to school earlier than she had, so they would have had time to plan something really vicious to greet her.

Stevie walked quickly, but it wasn't easy since she spent the entire trip looking over her shoulder, wondering when the retaliation would hit. But there was nothing. No sign of any brothers, no sign of any trouble. That made her even more nervous.

"Hi, missed you this morning!" Chad said cheerfully, dashing to his first class as Stevie entered the school.

Stevie waved and smiled in return. That was odd. Chad usually didn't say anything to her, much less something nice.

Before she had a chance to worry about that too much, Alex tapped her on her shoulder. "Hey, I picked up your Spanish workbook by mistake. Sorry about that, but when I checked the work you'd done last night, I saw you made a few mistakes. I corrected them for you. Okay?" He shoved the book into her hands and dashed off to his first class.

Expecting the worst, Stevie opened her workbook to see what he'd done. She was surprised to find that he'd done exactly what he'd said he'd done. She had forgotten to make her adjectives and nouns agree. He'd made them all agree. Stevie was astonished. Her Spanish teacher would be, too.

Stevie had three classes before the midmorning break, the first time she saw Michael that day at school. She wanted to buy herself an apple at the snack cart, but she'd been in such a hurry that she'd left her wallet at home.

"Here, I've got a quarter you can have," Michael said when he saw his sister's problem.

"You do?"

"Sure," he said, handing it to her.

"Do you want me to sign an IOU or something?" Stevie asked.

"Nah," Michael said. "I trust you."

Stevie was speechless. She accepted the quarter and bought the apple, thinking all the while about the hundreds of IOUs Michael had made her sign for him over the years.

Something was up.

One of Stevie's classmates came up to her while she was chewing thoughtfully on her apple.

"Wasn't that your brother?" the girl asked. Stevie nodded. "The one who wears Spiderman underwear?" Stevie nodded again. "He's so sweet!" Stevie nodded once more. "So how could you do something so mean to a little boy who is so sweet?" the girl asked.

Stevie gave her a withering look. "He's not always that sweet. And besides, I think the reason he gave me the money for the apple is to see that I stay healthy. See, I already owe him over twenty-three dollars. He sees this as protecting an investment." Stevie tossed the remains of the apple into a garbage can and headed for science. It was going to be easier to look at the insides of a frog than to figure out what her brothers were really up to.

"WHAT'S THE MATTER with you?" Lisa asked Carole as they stood next to one another in the outfield of a softball game. Carole had such a pained look on her face that it was clear she would be unable to catch the merest pop fly, much less a tricky line drive.

"It's Stevie," she said.

"I thought so," Lisa replied.

"Look, even though her brothers didn't say or do anything last night when we were at her house doesn't mean that they aren't ever going to do or say anything to Stevie in retaliation."

"I'm afraid you're right."

"I *am* right," Carole said. "After all, they *are* Stevie's brothers, and her skills at practical jokes and revenge are so well developed that they had to come from somewhere. I mean, you can't just *learn* that kind of stuff. It's born in you." Carole glanced up. "Why is that boy waving at me?" she asked.

There was a *thump* as a softball landed on the ground in front of Carole.

"That's why," Lisa said. She picked up the ball and tossed it toward the infield, totally oblivious to the classmate of hers who was dashing madly for third base. "But back to Stevie, remember the time Chad got so tired of Stevie not putting her laundry away that he washed all of her riding clothes with too much bleach?"

"Exactly!" Carole said. "Her jeans were white, and her breeches got all shredded because they were made of synthetics."

"And her mother was so mad at Chad for ruining all those expensive clothes that she made him wear his underwear, even though it had turned pink when Stevie washed it with her new T-shirt."

"We just *heard* about the underwear," Carole reminded her. "But everybody could *see* the pink socks."

"He wasn't a very good sport about it, was he?"

Thump! Another ball landed nearby. Carole moved aside so another classmate could run over and pick it up. Talking about Stevie seemed a lot more important than playing softball.

"And that was just the laundry wars," Carole said. "Remember the time Alex took Stevie's book report and handed it in, saying it was his?"

"Who could forget?" Stevie asked. "Stevie was so angry that she took a book report Michael had gotten a poor grade on and handed it in to the same teacher with Alex's name on it—for extra credit?"

"And remember the time Stevie accidentally dropped a piece of bubble gum on Chad's pillow when she was listening to his tape deck, and he got so angry that he stuck a wad of bubble gum on her pillow, and Mrs. Lake had to cut Stevie's hair off so she could get to school without the pillow attached?"

"Yes, I remember that one, too."

"None of this is making me feel any better," Carole said. "This is a family of vindictive practical jokers."

"I know," Lisa said. "But what can we do about it?"

Thump!

Nothing was going right.

STEVIE GOT A sinking feeling right before lunchtime. It came from her vivid recollection of the nice brown lunch bag she'd seen on the kitchen counter that morning as she'd flown by it on the way out to school.

She slunk into the cafeteria and sat glumly at her usual place. She stared at the empty table in front of her. She tried to imagine what a nice bologna-and-cheese sandwich would taste like—if she had one. She thought about the nice Cranapple juice she was sure her mother had put into the lunch bag—at home. She closed her eyes and dreamed about the sweet red grapes—that were just getting warm and soft on the kitchen counter. This was no fun at all.

"What happened? Where's your lunch?"

Stevie looked up. It was Alex. She shrugged. "I left it at home," she said.

"Oh, that's too bad," Alex said. "Let's see what your brothers can do for you." He disappeared.

Here it comes, she told herself. She decided that this was when they would get even. One of them would get something really disgusting—maybe even from the biology lab—and would pretend it was delicious. Another might even find a half-eaten dessert from the garbage. And to drink? She didn't even want to think about it.

"Oh, hi, Stevie!" a familiar and unwelcome voice said sweetly. It was Veronica diAngelo. Just what she needed on an empty stomach. Veronica pulled out a chair and sat down next to Stevie. This wasn't like Veronica. She usually steered very far from Stevie, and that was usually just fine with Stevie. Now her brothers were being nice, and Veronica was being friendly. Her whole world was turning upside down.

"Hello, Veronica," Stevie returned.

"Can I ask a question?" Veronica said.

"You just did—and that's your limit," Stevie said.

She knew that sounded really rude, but Veronica was really rude, and Stevie wasn't in the mood for her.

Veronica laughed sweetly, the tinkling sound of her giggles filling the air. Stevie couldn't believe it.

"You're so funny!" Veronica said.

Stevie simply stared at her.

"What I wanted to ask you was what happened between you and your brothers? I mean you guys are fighting all the time, but what did they do to you that was so bad you decided to put up those signs in the girls' room?"

"It's a family matter, Veronica," Stevie said. There was no way she was going to tell Veronica about the teasing she and Phil had gotten from her brothers.

Veronica was about to speak, and Stevie knew what she was going to say: How could anything that resulted in public signs in the girls' room be considered a private matter? Instead of listening, Stevie turned her back to Veronica.

Another classmate and a Pine Hollow rider, Lorraine Olson, sat down next to her.

"What's up between you and your brothers?" Lorraine asked.

Stevie was only too happy to explain it to her—a particularly nice snub for Veronica, who was still sitting right there, to hear Stevie tell the whole story to somebody else when she'd been unwilling to share any of it with Veronica. Maybe this lunch period wasn't going to be so bad after all.

She'd just gotten to the part about their making fun of a mock hunt when Alex arrived.

"Here you go, Stevie," he said, offering her a lunch bag.

"Thanks," she said, accepting it because she was curious to see if he had actually managed to talk the biology teacher into donating something that had been soaking in formaldehyde for months. Alex disappeared into the crowd. Stevie peered into the bag.

It held a sandwich—clearly bologna and cheese on white with mayonnaise, just the way she liked it. That was the way Michael liked it, too, so it had to be his sandwich. There was also some apple juice. She would have preferred Cranapple, but Chad's drink was apple juice. This was his drink container. Unopened. Then there was a large orange. Alex always had an orange in his lunch. Stevie crinkled her eyebrows in confusion. Each one of her brothers had contributed something he really liked to her lunch. Each one of them had done something very nice for her. That was odd—very odd.

Stevie opened the sandwich and the apple juice and began eating slowly, thinking about the very weird things that were going on. Around her, her friends talked about other things: the history test coming up next week; the Emerson Circus; and the fox hunt.

Stevie concentrated all her thoughts on her brothers. They'd been mean to her and Phil, and she'd been very angry with them. She'd gotten even. And now that they were even, her brothers were being nice to her, saying they got her joke and didn't want her to play any more practical jokes on them. That's what being even meant.

Stevie was pretty sure she understood now. After all, they were her brothers and they were a good lot, even if they were sometimes hard to take. Brothers and sisters had to stick together most of the time, and the Lakes were all good brothers and sister. There was nothing to worry about at all.

Or was there?

"ISN'T THIS WONDERFUL?" Carole asked Stevie and Lisa. Her friends had to agree. In spite of the fact that it was seven-thirty in the morning, it was definitely wonderful. They were at Pine Hollow, and the riders from Cross County had just arrived, accompanying vans filled with their own ponies and horses. Everywhere anybody looked, there were horses and riders, tack and equipment. There was a flurry of activity, riders tacking up, grooms grooming, mothers and fathers delivering unnecessary instruction, and Max and Mr. Baker scurrying around. Both carried clipboards and were busily making notes about everything they saw—and didn't see.

"I can't wait for it all to begin," Lisa said.

Carole looked around and smiled. "It already has

begun," she said. "Remember that riding is more than being on a horse. It's also taking care of the horse and preparing for being on the horse. . . ."

Sometimes Carole could be almost too serious about horseback riding. When that happened, her friends thought it was their responsibility to remind her about it. "Oh come on, Carole," Stevie teased. "We know that as well as you do. But the mock hunt won't really begin until we're all here and on our horses. *That's* what Lisa and I can't wait for."

"Me, neither," Carole admitted graciously.

The three girls had been at Pine Hollow for more than half an hour. They were each dressed in proper hunt attire, which meant that they were wearing riding pants and boots, white shirts and ties, and jackets, as well as their usual safety helmets. Their horses were tacked up and ready to go. Carole was riding her own horse, Starlight. Stevie was on Topside, the show horse she usually rode. At her friends' suggestion, and with Max's approval, Lisa had agreed to try Diablo, the tall bay gelding who had gotten his name because of his unusually small pointed ears.

While the three of them were all ready to go, it seemed that nobody else around them was—or for that matter ever would be. Everywhere was mass confusion.

"Isn't that my saddle?"

"The horse tried to bite me!"

"Where's my horse?"

"Does anybody have a crop I can borrow?"

The Saddle Club secured their horses to the paddock fence and joined the fray. They figured that if they helped the other riders get ready, it might actually speed up the entire process so they could begin the mock hunt sooner. It seemed to work. Within about fifteen minutes, just about everything was done for all the riders.

There were more than forty Pony Clubbers from Horse Wise and Cross County who were there for the mock hunt. The Saddle Club thought it was exciting just to see so many riders all saddled up and ready to go at once. Stevie looked over her shoulder. Phil was behind her. He smiled at her. She winked at him. That made him smile some more.

"Pony Clubs come to order!" Mr. Baker commanded. Everybody was quiet. Then Max spoke.

"I am now ready to assign parts to all of you," he began. He explained that most people were going to be in the field, but that some would have special jobs. "First of all, we need a Junior Master of the Hunt. This job is going to the person who has been the most serious student of fox hunting—the person who worked hardest at understanding all the aspects of it."

Me? Stevie wondered. No way. Carole? Not really. Carole knew a lot about hunting, but she hadn't worked all that hard to study it now. Lisa? Of course.

". . . and that is Lisa Atwood."

Most of the members of Horse Wise clapped politely. Stevie and Carole were much more raucous about it. Stevie even cheered.

"Then we need to have a huntsman. I conferred with Mr. Baker on this and chose one of his riders, Phil Marston." The members of Cross County clapped. Stevie cheered again.

Max named five whippers-in, including Carole, and told them that they would be working closely with Phil. That was good, because though Phil was a good rider, he wasn't so familiar with the land around Pine Hollow, and he'd need Carole's help to figure out where the fox could be hiding.

". . . and now we come to the fox. For this, we needed to find somebody who could be wily, clever, devious, cunning, sneaky, shrewd, sly, and deceitful." He paused. Stevie took the opportunity to look around and was surprised to see that absolutely everybody was looking straight at her.

Carole clapped her hand over her mouth to try to contain her giggles, but it was no good. They simply exploded. Lisa joined in, and within seconds, all forty riders were laughing.

Stevie blushed bright red.

"*Moi?*" she asked, trying to sound innocent.

"If the shoe fits," Max said, himself laughing. "Now, next is the matter of where we can ride and where we can't ride. Stevie and most of the Pine Hollow riders are familiar with the land that we can use. I have made a small map for each rider to carry—"

Max was interrupted by the sound of a car door slamming and a familiar voice shouting, "Re-ed! I need your help! Where are you?"

It was Veronica. She'd arrived late and now expected Red O'Malley, Pine Hollow's head stable hand, to help her groom Garnet and tack up.

A pained look crossed Max's face. Mr. Baker seemed a little confused. "One more rider," Max explained.

Red excused himself from the group and went to tack up Garnet. Veronica seemed to think he could do it very well without any help from her, so she joined the riders and waited for Red to bring Garnet to her. That was very typical of Veronica, and if Max hadn't thought it was more important right then for her to hear what he was going to say, he would have shooed her into the stable and told Red to leave her to her own devices.

"As I was saying," he continued, "I have made up a map which all the riders should carry with them. There are a few farmers who have specifically asked us not to ride on their land, either because they simply don't want us there or because they still have some crops in the ground. We must always respect their wishes. Not only would it be trespassing to disobey, but it would also jeopardize the permission we've received from other landowners. In other words, don't break this rule. Do you understand?"

Everybody nodded. All of Pine Hollow's riders had had this basic rule of riding pounded into them from the first time they'd ever been on horseback. Everybody understood and agreed.

"Okay, then, I think it's about time for our fox to get going, so all you animals, come get your ears."

Stevie thought the ears were just a little bit silly as she saw some of the kids designated as "hounds" put them on. However, when she saw her own "fox" ears, she changed her mind completely. They were adorable!

Proudly she slipped the ears on over her helmet and adjusted them until she was pretty sure they were straight. When Phil saw her with her ears on, he whistled.

"That's a wolf whistle," she joked. "Totally wrong for a fox."

"Well, let's see just how good a fox you are," he told her. "I can promise you, you haven't got a chance against a really terrific huntsman such as myself."

Stevie grinned. She loved nothing better than a good contest, and she could tell that this would certainly be that. "We'll see," she said evasively. "We'll just see."

48

On that note, she mounted Topside and walked him over to where Max was waiting for her.

"This is right up your alley," Max said. "I know you'll be a great fox."

"I hope so," Stevie said.

"Don't worry. You're a natural. Now, here's what you want to do. . . ."

He explained that she had two jobs. The first and most obvious was to try to avoid capture by the huntsman and the hounds. Max suggested that she try to think of a way to make all the other riders think she had gone one way while she actually went another. Stevie's mind was racing already. Max was right. This job was tailor-made for her. Her other job, and really the more important one in a way, was to lead everybody on a ride that would be fun.

"That's what this is about," he said.

"Fun is my middle name," Stevie said.

"Sometimes I think it's your first and last names, too," Max told her. Stevie wasn't absolutely sure that was a compliment, but she decided that for present purposes it was pretty good.

"I'm going to keep all the riders in the stable while you get a ten-minute head start." Then he handed her a bag of confetti. He told her it was her "scent." To be fair to the huntsman and the hounds, she had to drop a small handful of "scent" every five minutes. "Of course, they won't necessarily know when you dropped

49

it, or in what order the handfuls were dropped," he said. "You can use those facts to confuse them as much as you want."

"Oh, I intend to do that," she promised, a wicked grin crossing her face. Then she solemnly shook Max's hand and told him good-bye. As soon as he was inside the stable, she dropped her first handful of confetti and headed for the woods.

"WELL, THEN, IF I can't be the Junior Master, I'll be the huntsman," Veronica announced.

"Phil is the huntsman," Carole told her. "If you had managed to be here on time, you would have known that. You are a rider in the field. Nothing more, nothing less."

"We'll see about that," Veronica said. She spun on her heels and made a beeline for Max and Mr. Baker, who were guarding the door to the stable so that nobody could see where Stevie had gone.

"What's the matter with her?" Phil asked Carole.

"She thinks that just because she comes from a wealthy family, she ought to be in charge of everything. She wants your job, and unless I've sadly misjudged the situation, she is now going to ask Max and Mr. Baker to remove you as huntsman and install her in the position."

Phil and Carole watched. They couldn't hear what was being said, but they could see the surprised look on Mr. Baker's face as Veronica tried to make her case. She was gesturing toward her own breeches and riding jacket.

"You know what she's doing?" Carole asked.

Phil shook his head. "I couldn't possibly guess."

"She's showing Mr. Baker and Max that she's perfectly dressed for a hunt, and she's telling them that you are not. Therefore, *she* should be the huntsman."

They couldn't see Veronica's face as Mr. Baker and Max answered, but Carole was quite certain she knew what was being said and how Veronica was reacting.

"Max just told her that the huntsman is a person on horseback, not a clotheshorse, and that it's a job given to somebody responsible, who arrives on time, tacks up his or her own horse, and who can be counted on to be a leader. . . ."

"I don't think they said that much," Phil said, watching Veronica's every move. "She walked away too soon. But you probably covered the high points."

Lisa came over to Carole and Phil. "I don't believe what Veronica just did," she said.

"Believe it," Carole said. "The girl will never change."

Carole saw Max look at his watch, wait for a moment, and then look up. "Riders up!" he called out. It was now time to try to figure out just how clever Stevie was going to be today. Carole hoped Stevie would be in top form.

The mock hunt had been organized very much like the real thing, and the participants were expected to act their parts just as they would in a real hunt. Therefore, Lisa took the lead, along with Mr. Baker, who was serving as the grown-up Master.

Lisa instructed Phil to get the hounds in order and to see if they could pick up the "line," or scent of the fox.

The whippers-in stayed at the edge of the pack of five hounds, and Phil told the hounds when to begin the hunt.

It took only a few seconds to find the first pile of scent. That was easy. The question, then, was what direction Stevie had taken from the back of Pine Hollow.

"That way," Lisa suggested, pointing to the section of woods nearby. Something—most likely a horse—had made a trail in the grass leading toward the woods that way.

Phil didn't move. He jutted his lower jaw forward thoughtfully. "That would be logical," he said. "But we're not talking logical. We're talking Stevie. Let's go *that* way first." He pointed to a section of woods across a series of fields separated by wooden fences with gates through them. The whole section was crisscrossed with horse-made trails. "She would know that would be much more confusing for us."

"But all those gates!" Lisa said, imagining how long it would take Stevie to open and close each one of them.

"She's riding Topside," Phil reminded Lisa. "Topside is a championship show horse. He can jump most of those fences. We don't have a minute to waste."

"Tallyho, then," Lisa declared, and the hunt began.

6

Stevie clucked her tongue, urging Topside to hurry through the woods. She wanted to lay this part of her trail as quickly as possible, dropping her confetti "scent" often to confuse the huntsman and the hounds.

Stevie didn't often have a chance to ride all by herself. Although she loved being with friends, it was kind of nice to be alone with Topside. It made her imagination churn, thinking what it might have been like for pioneers to ride through these woods alone hundreds of years ago, not knowing which tree might hide a predator or an enemy. That made her feel a lot like a fox. It was a real inspiration.

"Now what are we going to do?" she asked Topside. His ears flicked around at the sound of her voice, but he didn't seem to have an answer. Stevie was going to have to do this all by herself. She drew Topside to a halt, sprinkled some confetti on the ground, and thought.

She was near a hillside, not far from Willow Creek, and headed for farmland where they were not supposed to ride. The hillside seemed the most logical move. There were a lot of hiding places there, and years of riding horseback in the woods and playing hide-and-seek there with her riding friends had taught Stevie where every one of them was. Those years had also taught Carole, and then Lisa, where the hiding places were, too. There were some caves, some brush-covered areas, some gullies, all of which afforded ample opportunity for hiding. Carole and Lisa knew every single one of them. Stevie realized then that if the hounds and huntsman got into this section of the woods, they would spend a very long time looking in every single hiding place. That would be absolutely wonderful for a wily fox, especially if that wily fox were *not* in any of those hiding places.

"What a great idea!" Stevie told Topside, her face lighting up with joy. "Let's get going!"

With that, Stevie headed toward the hillside, where she knew all the hiding places were. She dropped some confetti, followed the trail up the hillside, and dropped some more. Then she began her clever ruse. She turned Topside around and followed her trail back-

ward, exactly. She passed the place where she had
dropped the confetti, and then she dropped some
more. The hounds and the huntsman would see the
confetti, but they would have no idea that she was actually heading *down* the hill, rather than up it, when
she dropped that particular handful of "scent."

The next trick was to get to the creek before she had
to drop any more confetti. She intended to go into the
creek and stay there, following it all the way back to
the field, once the other riders were out of the field.
While she was in the creek, she was safe as safe could
be. Oh, she'd drop all the confetti she had to, but it
would float downstream in the water, well away from
where any of the other riders would see it. In fact, she
could drop the whole bag, and it wouldn't tell anybody
anything about where she was.

Stevie beamed proudly. She was a very clever fox,
indeed.

They reached Willow Creek safely before Stevie had
to drop any more confetti. Topside lowered himself
into the shallow water, and Stevie let him have a re-
freshing drink. Then, hearing the approaching riders,
Stevie clucked her tongue, signaled with her legs and
seat, and got Topside moving through the water. Topside liked walking in the creek. Even though it was
cool weather and the water was surely chilly, Topside
moved forward quietly and willingly. Stevie loved the
sound of the horse's hooves slooshing through the

water and his shoes clicking surely against the rocks in the creek bed. It was a wonderful sound, and every single step took her farther and farther from those who were hunting her.

"I FOUND SOMETHING!" Anna McWhirter announced. "It think it's confetti."

"It isn't," Lisa said, examining it closely. "It looks like a bubble-gum wrapper to me."

"Does Stevie chew bubble gum?" Anna asked.

"Sometimes, but she would never drop a wrapper in the woods. Look for confetti."

Thirty-nine to one seemed to Lisa to be a pretty good set of odds, unless of course the "one" was Stevie Lake. Lisa wasn't at all sure she was happy to be the Junior Master of this hunt. A fox was one thing—Stevie was another. Stevie would do everything she could to win this game, and Lisa was beginning to think that that might involve making her and all the other riders look a little silly. Lisa didn't like looking silly.

"Phil, can't you get those hounds to find the confetti?" she said.

"I'm doing my best," he said. "But you know Stevie. She's going to do something totally unpredictable."

Lisa sighed. "I know," she said. "That's what I'm afraid of, too."

"I bet she's heading for cover," Phil told Lisa. "Are there any hiding places around here?"

"That's *it*!" Lisa said. Then she signaled for Carole to join them. Carole left the group of "hounds" she had been trying to get to search for "scent" and rode over to Lisa and Phil.

"We've got to put our heads together," Lisa said. "We think the fox has gone to cover, and you know there are a zillion hiding places on the hillside. How do we start?"

"Of course!" Carole said, agreeing with Lisa and Phil. "I remember all the times we played hide-and-seek, but if she's hiding, we've got an awful lot of seeking to do."

"This calls for organization," Phil said. He looked at Lisa. He knew her reputation for logical thinking.

Lisa paused for a moment. Phil and Carole could practically see the thinking process.

"We're going to have to divide the hillside area into sectors and assign hounds to each sector until we find some 'scent.' When we've narrowed down the area, then Carole and I can tell you where the best hiding places are."

Carole looked around quizzically. "Where's Veronica?" she asked.

"Beats me," Lisa said. "The last I saw of her, she'd decided that Garnet wouldn't like going into the woods. She said something about waiting out in the fields until we all came to our senses."

Phil seemed confused.

"Veronica doesn't like riding in the woods," Carole explained. "She might get scratched by a branch or something. It's just like Veronica to try to make it Garnet's fault."

"With that girl, everything is somebody else's fault, isn't it?" Phil said.

"It doesn't matter," Lisa said. "The fact is that a hunt without Veronica is actually better than one with her. If she were here with us, she'd have some kind of imaginary problem that would make it harder for all of us. Frankly, I was expecting Garnet to have a loose shoe before we got to the woods. If she's happy waiting in the field for us to return victoriously with Stevie, that's okay with me."

"Me, too," Carole agreed. "So let's forget about Veronica and concentrate on Stevie."

Then there was a very odd sound. It was a sort of mangled holler, a little bit like a dog yowling, only there weren't any dogs around. It had to be one of the "hounds."

"Methinks the hounds have found the line!" Phil said excitedly.

Lisa's eyes brightened, too. "Okay, then, we can narrow it down to one sector right now. See? Hunting really is easy as long as you try to think logically," she said proudly.

"I hope you're right," Phil said. "But remember, this is Stevie we're dealing with."

"Sure, but don't forget that Stevie's dealing with three of her best friends—and it takes three to know one!"

STEVIE AND TOPSIDE paused, standing in the cool running water of Willow Creek. Stevie knew the creek was about to enter the open field and she'd have no more cover in a few steps. She had to be absolutely certain that the field was empty before she left the woods for the open. She could hear the babbling of the water. She could hear some late season creatures rustling in the short grass. She could see the wind blow the remaining yellow stalks, and she could smell the cool freshness of the early-morning dew. There were a lot of things going on in the open field, but there wasn't a sign of the hunters. She was home free.

Cautiously and slowly, she moved forward, Topside's hooves in a muted clip-clop on wet rocks. She stopped again and looked around once more. She saw nothing. Pine Hollow's stable was across three fields—a distance of perhaps three-quarters of a mile. All she had to do was get across those three fields without being spotted. That meant she was going to have to go fast.

She reached into the confetti bag and fished out a handful of paper flakes. She dropped them onto the ground and began her dash. If she could get inside the paddock and through the stable door, she could win. It was an inspiring thought.

Topside had been raised to perform. He felt the urgency in Stevie's signals to him and he spurted into action, moving quickly from a trot to a canter and then into a genuine gallop. It was a glorious gait. Stevie loved the feeling of the wind lifting her long hair and brushing it back. She scooted across the first field, approached the fence, leaned forward, rose in her saddle, and signaled Topside to jump. He fairly flew. As soon as Topside recovered from the jump, she aimed him toward the second fence. That was when she realized that she couldn't go that way. It led straight across some land belonging to a man named Andrews that the riders did not have permission to use. The detour was going to be a time-consuming nuisance, but though Stevie was only too happy to break most rules, this was one she always followed scrupulously. She'd have to find another route. She turned Topside sharply to the right and skirted the Andrews land, turning left at the end of the fence. Finally, she turned right and was once again aimed for the stable. All she had to do was—

"Help!"

Stevie thought she heard something.

"Help!!"

She definitely heard something. She shortened Topside's reins and sat down in the saddle. The horse drew to a walk. Stevie stood up in the stirrups so she could look to see where the cry came from.

"Where are you?"

"Here!"

Stevie turned. There, sitting in the grass with tears streaking down her cheeks, was one of Pine Hollow's young riders, May Grover.

Stevie and Topside hurried over to May. As soon as she reached the little girl, she dismounted. "What happened?" she asked.

"My pony threw me," May said, rubbing the place that hurt the most—her seat. "One of the big girls was supposed to look after me, but she just rode on. She didn't even notice."

Stevie didn't have to ask which "big girl" that was. May's description clearly applied to only one "big girl." That was Veronica diAngelo.

Stevie crouched down and examined May carefully. She could tell that the little girl had hurt herself, but it was even clearer that the part of her that hurt the most was her feelings. May stifled her snuffles and her tears while Stevie looked her over. When Stevie was convinced nothing was broken and standing up would be good for May, she helped the little girl to her feet.

"Where's your pony?" Stevie asked.

"Luna ran away!" she wailed. The tears started spouting out again. "I'll never catch him—and I really, really love him!"

Stevie gave May a great big hug. "Don't worry," she said. "I'll find him for you. He won't go very far—not as long as he knows there's going to be some good breakfast for him soon. Let's see if Topside can help us find Luna, okay?"

"Would you do that for me?" May asked.

"Of course," Stevie said.

"But you're the fox!"

Stevie had been so concerned about May that she'd almost forgotten that fact. When she'd left Pine Hollow that morning, it had seemed to her that the most important thing in the world was outfoxing the other riders. Now, she realized, taking care of May was actually higher up on the priority list. Besides, who was to say she couldn't do both at the same time?

"I've got an idea," Stevie said. "You know foxes sometimes travel in pairs, don't you?"

"Max says two foxes are called a brace of foxes."

"You've been studying," Stevie accused her.

May smiled. "I wanted to know everything," she explained. "I like to know everything."

"Then you'll make a great partner for me," Stevie said. With that, she climbed back into Topside's saddle and then reached down, offering May her left arm for a boost. Stevie took her left foot out of the stirrup, and by using her arm and the stirrup, May was able to climb on board. She sat comfortably in front of Stevie in Topside's saddle.

It took Stevie only a few minutes to figure out that May's pony was hiding behind a small stand of trees where some sweet grass remained uncut. Stevie picked up the pony's reins. One look at him, and she knew why he'd been named Luna. He was a bay with a perfect half-moon on his face. She clucked her tongue, and the pony came along obediently.

Just before they reached the paddock, something made Stevie look back over her shoulder. What she saw was none other than Veronica diAngelo, waving wildly and screaming triumphantly at Stevie and May.

"Wouldn't you know it?" Stevie said.

"That's the girl who was supposed to take care of me," May said. "Now it looks like somebody ought to take care of her. What's wrong with her?"

"She just thinks she's so smart because she saw us first. That's why she's waving her arms."

"I didn't mean that part," May said. "What's wrong with her that she's riding across Mr. Andrews's field?"

May was absolutely right, and it was the best news Stevie had all day. She gave May a big squeeze. "You're quite a fox!" Stevie declared.

USUALLY STEVIE FOUND it quite boring when she had to walk her horse to cool him down after a ride. She and May were circling the indoor ring at Pine Hollow on foot, leading Topside and May's pony, Luna. They walked quietly so they could hear every word Max and Mr. Baker were saying to Veronica. There was nothing boring about it.

"Veronica, you are very familiar with the rules," Max said.

"But I saw Stevie. I just had to catch up to her."

"It wasn't your job to catch up to her. That's the huntsman's job. It was your job to inform the huntsman that you'd seen her."

"Well, she shouldn't have been where she was, and there was no way I could have told anybody else. If

67

she'd been in the woods where any sensible fox would have been, it wouldn't have been any problem. Instead, she was dashing for home—and stopped to help that little girl—"

"Who you were supposed to be looking out after," Max interrupted. Veronica ignored that.

"—so I did the most logical thing because I was so much closer than anyone else," Veronica protested.

"The riders on a hunt are along to watch, not to do the work of others," Mr. Baker said sternly. "The fox-hunting rules are well-known and well-established. If participants don't follow the rules, there will be chaos. By following the fox on your own instead of informing the Master and the huntsman, you made a serious breach of fox-hunting etiquette. It cannot be permitted."

Veronica gave him a look that Stevie had seen before many times. It was a look that said, "I hear what you're saying and I don't agree with you, but I'm going to pretend that I do just so you'll stop complaining."

What her mouth said was, "I'm sorry. It won't happen again."

"You're right about that," Mr. Baker said. "And it certainly won't happen in any hunt that I have anything to do with. Turning around and getting ahead of the huntsman and the Master was thoughtless and rude, but crossing Mr. Andrews's land was simply unforgivable. As of now, Max is withdrawing his invitation to you to participate further in this mock hunt, and I am formally disinviting you to the junior hunt at Cross County next week."

"You—what?" Veronica exploded. Nobody had ever disinvited her to anything. After all, she considered herself to be from one of the finest families. Veronica simply couldn't believe her ears.

"Good-bye," Mr. Baker said. He turned his back to her.

Stevie could hardly believe her ears or her eyes either. It was too wonderful. She could have imagined dozens of ways to play tricks and try to get back at Veronica, but not one of them could possibly measure up to what Mr. Baker had done with a few sharp words. As far as fox hunting went, Veronica was history.

"Isn't it great?" Stevie whispered to May.

May nodded conspiratorially. "She deserves it."

The girls gave one another high fives. Max glanced up sharply when he heard the clap of their hands. Without further ado, the girls returned to the job of cooling down their horses. The last thing they wanted was to draw the attention of Max and Mr. Baker when they were in any kind of disinviting mood. Their worry turned out to be unnecessary.

"Looks like those horses might be ready for a rest now," Mr. Baker said. "Why don't you girls—I mean foxes—dig into the hunt breakfast?"

"As long as nobody's serving fox!" May said.

"Don't worry," Stevie assured her. "I think the main course is crow." She just couldn't take her eyes off Veronica, who appeared to be slinking out of the ring.

As usual, Veronica had forgotten all about Garnet. She'd left her horse standing alone in the middle of the ring with his reins trailing on the ground. Max was about to yell after her.

"Don't bother," Stevie said. "It's not worth it and she won't learn anything from it. May and I will put Garnet away along with Topside and Luna. Then we can really enjoy our breakfast and wait for the frustrated hunters to return."

"Thanks, Stevie," Max said.

Together the girls took the horses back to the stalls. They would have time to do a complete grooming later. For now, they just wanted to remove the horses' tack, give them some well-deserved water and hay, and let them rest.

Stevie carried Topside's and Garnet's tack to the tack room. On the way back from there, she passed a window that opened onto the driveway of Pine Hollow and the street beyond it.

Veronica was standing by the edge of the road. Stevie figured she was probably waiting for her mother, or the chauffeur, to pick her up. It was only a fifteen-minute walk to Veronica's house, but that was always too much for Little Miss Perfect. In spite of the fact that Veronica had just been totally humiliated by Max and Mr. Baker, she stood tall with her nose in the air. Stevie mused about what she saw and decided that Veronica was one of a kind—fortunately. Then, as she watched, something very curious happened. Her brother, Chad, happened by, on his bicycle. Veronica waved hello to him, and he drew his bicycle to a stop. Whatever else could be said about Veronica—and there was a lot—she was a pretty girl. Chad never failed to notice a pretty girl who waved at him.

"You two deserve one another," Stevie told the pair, though of course they couldn't hear her. Just to prove her point, she slammed the window shut. They couldn't hear that, either. Stevie didn't care. She picked up three flakes of hay and took them to Topside, Garnet, and Luna. Then it was time for everybody to have breakfast.

Stevie and May were into their second helpings of bagels and cream cheese when the first shouts came from outside the stable.

"Here's some more confetti!"

"No, it *can't* be! She must have dropped that on the way out!"

"No way! It wasn't here before. I just know it."

"It wasn't. Definitely." That was Phil's voice. "I'm telling you. She's done the sneakiest thing possible! She's inside right now eating a bowl of cereal."

Stevie grinned uncontrollably. She turned to May. "And they think they know me. Shows how much he knows if he thinks I'd have cereal when there are bagels around!"

May giggled.

"Are you sure?" Lisa asked. "There are still dozens of hiding places on that hillside that we haven't even begun to explore."

"Woof! Woof!" one of the pretend hounds barked.

"What are you barking about?" Carole asked.

"That," the "hound" said, pointing. All the riders looked where she pointed. What they saw was the window to Topside's stall, and inside was Topside.

"She is a clever one!" Carole said proudly. "But I'll bet you she isn't eating cereal in there—"

"What do you mean?"

"She likes bagels best," Carole said.

"Ah, they do know me," Stevie said. With that, the doors to the inside ring burst open, and in came all of the Pony Club riders, led by Lisa and Phil, with the "hounds" milling at the head of the pack.

Stevie and May stood up and toasted the riders with orange juice.

"Gotcha!" Stevie said. Everybody laughed, and then Max began clapping.

When the cheering and congratulating died down, Max and Mr. Baker got the riders to cool their horses and put them in the stalls and vans. When the animals

were tended to, all the riders gathered at the breakfast table and helped themselves to the delicious
food.

Everyone began talking at once. First of all, the
hunters wanted to know what had happened to May
and Veronica. Stevie was only too happy to oblige and
filled them in on all the details. Max and Mr. Baker
tried to remain totally impassive while Stevie did
imitations of Veronica and Mr. Baker, but Max had
trouble stifling his laughter. Stevie was very good at
imitations and had, of course, remembered every word
spoken by Veronica and Mr. Baker. It was so funny
that soon all the young riders were laughing as well.
Stevie suspected that one of the reasons Mr. Baker let
her continue her imitation was that his disinvitation
to one young rider would serve as warning to anybody
who had any ideas about breaking hunt rules.

"So, enough about Veronica. Tell me what you all
did on the hunt while May and I did our part," Stevie
said.

"We chased you," Lisa said.

"Yeah, only what we ended up chasing was our own
shadows," Anna complained. "I think we searched
every single corner of that hillside."

"Oh, no," Carole assured her. "There are lots of hiding places we didn't even get near. Remember the gully
where the foal got stuck? And remember the time we

decided some pirates were hiding in a cave? And then there is the rock that juts out over the creek, where you tried to get Veronica to jump into the water?"

"Oh, right, where it's only about six inches deep?" Stevie said.

"That's the place," Carole said. "Anyway, we never began to look in any of those places."

"Too bad," Stevie said. "Because if you had, May and I would have had time for a nap before you got here! You must be really angry with me."

"Not at all," Phil said. "It's a great way to ride—not following a real trail, just following our instincts and being with our friends. We had a blast organizing ourselves into hunting parties so we could cover as much of the hillside as possible in as short a time as possible. It was fun!"

"It was?" Stevie asked. She'd hoped they'd all be just slightly angry with her for being so clever and making it impossible to hunt successfully.

Phil pulled out a chair and sat down next to Stevie. He put his arm across the back of her chair. "In fact," he said to her quietly, "the only thing that would have made it more fun was if you were along with us. I missed you." He smiled warmly. It made Stevie feel funny in her stomach—a nice kind of funny.

Stevie was never quite certain what to say when Phil said nice things like that. Probably the best thing was just to smile back. Still, she was a kidder, and she couldn't help herself.

"You sure did miss me!" she teased. Phil laughed. That was one of the things she really liked about him.

Lisa picked up a knife and began tapping it on her orange-juice glass. She stood up. "Attention, everybody, attention!" she ordered. There was quiet. She picked up her glass. "I would like to propose a toast," she began. "This is for the person who made this hunt so difficult—and so much fun." Everybody looked at Stevie. "To the cleverest, cagiest, wickedest fox there ever was."

"Brace of foxes," Stevie interrupted her, nodding acknowledgment to May.

"Brace of foxes," Lisa said, catching on quickly. May beamed proudly. "And all I can say is that I'm relieved to know that next week, on the junior hunt, we'll have a much easier task. There's no way a real fox can be as devious as this pair—unless, of course Stevie and May try to give them some pointers during the week!"

With that, she held her glass up to Stevie and then drank. Everybody joined in.

8

LISA WAS BUSY grooming Diablo inside his stall when the door slid open. The horse had gotten his coat very dirty in the course of the mock hunt, and there was a lot of work to do. She didn't want to be distracted from her work, but when she saw it was Carole, she relaxed. Carole entered and closed the door quietly behind her.

"We've got to do something," Carole said.

When the subject was horses, Carole was always as sharp as could be. When the subject was anything else, she had a tendency to be a bit flaky, and she didn't always make herself clear. Right then, Lisa didn't have any idea what she was talking about. She said so.

"It's Stevie," Carole said. "Not only is she in trouble with her brothers, but she's gotten Veronica even mad-

77

der at her. The girl's in trouble, big trouble, and she can't even admit it!"

Automatically Carole picked up a brush and began working on Diablo's coat. There was always so much work to be done around horses that all of Max's riders learned that if they wanted to talk, they'd have to do so as they worked.

"I was thinking," Carole went on, "that we should find a way to make up to the Lake boys so that they'll think it's Stevie apologizing to them."

"They'd never buy it," Lisa said, gently tugging the mane comb through Diablo's thick black mane. "Anybody who knows Stevie knows that the one thing she can't ever do is admit that she was wrong. They'll think it's some sort of hoax. No way."

"Then what?"

Lisa crinkled her brow. The person who was the best at figuring this sort of thing out was Stevie, and she was the one person they couldn't turn to. That meant they'd have to use their own strengths.

"Why don't we just talk to them?" Lisa suggested.

"Talk?" That wasn't what Carole had in mind at all.

"Yeah, talk. Maybe we can get them to agree to meet us somewhere and we can talk, you know, like lay our cards on the table."

"Won't that just let them know how worried we are and make them even more interested in getting back at Stevie?"

"Maybe," Lisa conceded. "However, it might also give us an idea of how serious they are at revenge—if we can read them right. The real question is, can it hurt? I don't think so."

"I don't know," Carole said. She exchanged the brush for a cloth and began rubbing Diablo's coat, bringing out a deep sheen. Lisa switched to his tail. The horse didn't flinch. He obviously loved the attention.

"I'll call them now," Lisa said. "Mrs. Reg isn't in her office. I'll use that phone."

"What about Stevie? Won't she overhear?" Carole asked.

"I don't think so. The last time I saw her, she was helping Phil load his horse onto a van, and he was talking about asking her to walk him over the path she'd taken this morning as the fox."

"Why would he want to walk all that distance in the woods?" Carole asked.

"I don't think he actually intends to," Lisa said. In fact, she was quite sure Phil and Stevie were just looking for an excuse to have a few minutes to themselves. Carole didn't seem to get it, though.

"But that's what he said, isn't it?" Carole persisted. "I'm sure Stevie must have ridden at least three or four miles, just trying to confuse us. Those two will be exhausted by the time—"

"Carole!" Lisa said, a little exasperated with her

friend. "Trust me. They aren't going to walk three or four miles. They're just going to walk into the woods a little way."

It was Carole's turn to look confused. "But I don't— ahh," she said, getting it at last. "Sure, that will give us plenty of time to call her brothers. Go for it!"

Lisa finished combing Diablo's tail, dropped the comb into her grooming bucket, and headed for Mrs. Reg's telephone.

Pine Hollow's riders were allowed to use the phone in cases of emergency. Lisa wasn't absolutely certain that Max would consider this an emergency, but Lisa did, and that was good enough for her.

The phone was picked up on the first ring. Alex answered it. Lisa was surprised at how readily Alex agreed to a meeting between the brothers and Lisa and Carole. Both Chad and Michael were also at home, and before Max even discovered that Lisa was on the phone, the date was made. The boys agreed to meet them at two-thirty behind the bait shop near the shopping center.

Lisa wasn't thrilled with the idea of the bait shop. It was a place that kept things like cut-up fish and live worms around for people to use to catch fish, and it stank to high heavens. Lisa tried to talk them into meeting someplace else—like, for instance, her house—but Alex pointed out that the bait shop was a place they could absolutely, positively guarantee Stevie would not see them. Lisa found that convincing and agreed. Besides, it would mean that they'd be near TD's, where they had made arrangements to meet Stevie at three o'clock. Lisa was certain that everything was going to work perfectly.

CAROLE PINCHED HER nostrils shut. "Uuoooof," she said distastefully.

"It's not so bad," Lisa said, a pained look on her face. "I mean, as long as you don't have to breathe in." She pinched her nose as well. Then she looked at her watch. It was two twenty-five. Arriving at the bait shop early had a major disadvantage in the smell department.

"Hi, Lisa, Carole. What's up?" It was Chad. Michael and Alex were right behind him. The meeting could begin.

First, though, Lisa insisted that they find a place to sit that was not right next to a barrel of chum. A little reluctantly, the boys agreed to move away. They found a rock nearby, close enough for there to be an awfully unpleasant odor, far enough so that Lisa and Carole could release their nostrils.

"It's about Stevie," Lisa began, getting right to the point. "We know that you guys were mean to her and to Phil last week, and then she got back at you at school by teasing you all publicly." She looked at each of the three boys as she spoke. When her eyes came to

Michael, however, it was impossible for her not to wonder if he was, actually, wearing Spiderman underwear. She tried not to let her face show it. Michael seemed to sense it however. He gave her a nasty look. Lisa took her eyes off Michael and looked at Alex. That was safer.

"I guess we all know that Stevie is quite the practical joker," she continued.

"Heh, heh, she sure is that," Alex agreed. Chad and Michael nodded.

"Sometimes a bit too much?" Lisa suggested. It was her first attempt at subtlety.

"Sometimes," Alex agreed. "But that's just Stevie's way."

"You don't mind?" Carole said, very surprised.

"Oh, living with Stevie's a howl," Chad said. "Just when you think things are calm, Stevie finds a way to mix them up, and there's always a big laugh involved. Life with Stevie is—is . . ."

He seemed to be searching for a word. Lisa thought she could supply it.

"Exciting?" she suggested.

"That's one way to put it," Alex agreed. "Fun is another."

"You mean you're not angry with her?" Carole asked.

The boys all looked at one another and shrugged.

"Angry?" Chad asked. "What about? Why would we be angry with her?"

"Oh, no particular reason," Lisa said, deciding on the spot it had been a terrible mistake to assume the boys were after revenge. She and Carole were just stirring things up—things that ought not to be stirred.

"Oh, we just love Stevie's practical jokes," Chad said. "They make life so interesting! Imagine how boring it would be if one of us could like a girl and know that there was no way anybody would interfere and try to make us look foolish. . . ."

Michael laughed. So did Alex. "Stevie's just Stevie," Alex assured Lisa and Carole. "She can be a pain in the neck, but you know we love her. We wouldn't do anything to hurt her. Is that what you were afraid of?"

"Sort of," Lisa admitted.

"No problem," Alex said. "The issue of the notes in the girls' room is long forgotten. There will be no revenge."

"You have our word," Chad promised.

"Mine, too," Michael agreed.

"Thanks," Carole said. "I guess we were just being silly, but with the hunt coming up, we were kind of afraid something was going to happen that might mess it up. We wouldn't want that to happen, we care about Stevie, you know."

"Oh, we do, too," Chad assured the girls. "We care about her a lot. We wouldn't ever let anything happen to our sister."

Lisa felt much better then. She and Carole had a straightforward promise from the boys that everything would be fine—especially with the hunt. She relaxed then for the first time in several hours.

"Speaking of the hunt, what was going on over at Pine Hollow this morning?" Chad asked. "I passed by, and I saw Veronica what's-her-name. It was some kind of pretend thing?"

Now Carole was on firm ground. She was always comfortable talking about anything that had to do with horses. She explained exactly what a mock hunt was and told the boys just how terrific their sister had been.

"She was better than any old real fox, I'm sure. She was just the perfect choice for a fox. She had us completely fooled."

"Oh, that's right up Stevie's alley," Alex agreed. "I bet she had a blast trying to outthink all of you!"

"She did," Lisa told him.

"Now, what's the difference between this and what's happening next week?" Chad asked.

Both Carole and Lisa were pleased with the interest Stevie's brothers were showing in the hunt. From what Stevie had said about the teasing she and Phil had received, Chad, Alex, and Michael weren't in the least bit interested in fox hunting. Lisa thought that maybe hearing about the mock hunt today had made them see how much fun it could actually be. The girls were only too happy to tell them all the details about fox hunting.

"You mean the dogs . . . ," Chad began.

"Hounds," Carole said. "They're never called dogs, always hounds."

"You mean the hounds can really smell where the fox has been?"

"They're trained hunting hounds," Lisa said. "They are raised to follow the scent."

"But what if there's no fox around?" Alex asked.

"Oh, but there is," Lisa said. "Mr. Baker knows that there are foxes on the land we'll be hunting next week. Sometimes, though, a hunt is held where there are no foxes. In those cases, people can still hunt, but they have something called a drag hunt, where the smell of a fox is laid on a path that the hounds and the huntsman and the riders can follow. It's not as much fun, but it's better than nothing. That doesn't matter, though, because we'll be after a real fox."

Michael made a face. "Will you kill it?"

"No way," Lisa promised him. "We probably won't even see it. Although the real fox won't be as clever as today's fox named Lake, it will still be fun to chase after it, and we're going to want it to be there the next time we want to chase it, too."

"Same way you feel about chasing after the fox named Lake?" Chad asked.

Lisa could tell that he was proud of what his sister had done. He had a right to be proud.

"Exactly the same," she promised him.

"That's what we wanted to hear," Chad said. Then he turned to his brothers. "Come on, guys. It's time to go home."

Lisa and Carole waved to them as they walked quickly toward their house.

"That wasn't so bad, was it?" Lisa asked Carole.

"Not at all," Carole said. "And now, having talked to them, I can't imagine why we thought there might be trouble. Stevie doesn't know how lucky she is to have such a nice set of brothers!"

Lisa looked at her watch. "Speaking of whom—let's get to TD's!"

The girls arrived at the ice-cream shop a few minutes later and found Stevie waiting for them in their favorite booth.

"How was your walk in the woods with Phil?" Carole asked.

Lisa nudged her. She didn't think that was a very good question.

"Better than your walk wherever you were," Stevie said, crinkling her nose. "Where have you been? You smell of fish. Ugh!"

"Fish?" Carole echoed innocently. "I can't imagine why."

Lisa gave her a withering look. They did both smell of fish. There was no way they could lie their way out of it.

"It's my fault," Lisa said. "We were taking a shortcut here from Pine Hollow and ended up near the bait shop. I was curious about the chum in the back of it. I made the terrible mistake of opening the barrel. Now it's going to take weeks to get this smell out of our clothes and hair."

"Remind me to stay away from you until then," Stevie said. "You smell like my brothers when they go fishing. Ugh."

"What'll it be, girls?" the waitress asked. When she saw Stevie, she paled. Stevie was famous for ordering outrageous combinations of ice cream and toppings.

"Just a dish of vanilla for me," Stevie said. "There are enough odd flavors and scents around here to turn my stomach already. Who needs the usual pistachios and cherries?"

The smell was getting to Lisa and Carole as well. They agreed on vanilla, too. Relieved, the waitress disappeared.

"And speaking of my brothers," Stevie said. "I've changed my mind. I'm now absolutely sure that they are going to try some kind of revenge on me—and it's going to be bad."

"What makes you think so?" Carole asked.

"It's just a feeling," Stevie said.

Lisa sighed contentedly to herself. For once, she was as sure about something as Stevie was, and this time what she was sure of was that Stevie was wrong.

"Oh, I wouldn't worry about it," Lisa said confidently. "If your brothers were going to get revenge, they would have done it already."

Stevie looked unconvinced, but she dropped the subject and dug into her ice cream. Across the table Lisa caught Carole's eye and gave her a conspiratorial wink.

9

CAROLE GAVE STARLIGHT a big hug before she took him out of his stall for his daily exercise on Monday. She loved doing special things on horseback, like the mock hunt and the upcoming junior hunt, but best of all, she just loved being with her horse, working with him and riding him. Any time she was with Starlight, it was special. Now, because of all the worry and confusion having to do with the hunt and Stevie, it seemed particularly nice to be doing nothing in particular with her horse.

"Let's go work on gait changes," Carole said. Starlight seemed to think that was a good idea.

It was raining out, so Max had given permission for them to work in the indoor ring. Lisa was already there. She and Carole had come directly from school as they usually did. Lisa was doing some work with Samson.

Samson was a young horse, born to a mare at the stable named Delilah. He was a coal black foal that the girls had helped deliver. They felt very close to him and were thrilled when Max had suggested that they could help with his training. He wasn't anywhere near ready to have riders on him yet, but that didn't mean it wasn't time to get him used to tack. The girls had already gotten him accustomed to the feel of a bit in his mouth. Now Lisa was trying out a saddle, without stirrups.

Carole walked Starlight to the entrance of the ring and mounted him just before she entered.

"How does Samson like the saddle?" Carole called.

Both Lisa and Samson looked up at her. "He almost doesn't seem to notice it," Lisa said. "I think he just thinks it's a heavier-than-normal blanket."

"Very good," Carole said. "That means that you've left the girth nice and loose."

"Just like you suggested," Lisa said. "When it comes to horses, you're always right."

"I wish that were so with people," Carole said. "They are much more complicated."

"That's for sure," Lisa agreed. She and Samson continued walking in large circles in the ring.

Carole walked Starlight around twice, allowing him

to warm up a bit. Then she put some pressure on his belly with her legs, and he began trotting. They would work on his schooling as soon as she was sure he was limber and ready. She had been riding for so long and had learned so much that it seemed she could feel every muscle in the horse when he moved. There was a very different feel to Starlight's gaits when he was warmed up than when he was still tense and stiff from a day and a night spent in his stall. By the third time he'd circled the large indoor ring, she could feel him relaxing. Part of it was the fact that he was just getting used to having Carole in the saddle. Part of it was that his muscles were now ready to work. So Carole put them to work.

She brought him back to a walk and then spent fifteen minutes systematically changing gaits, from walk to trot to canter to trot and back to canter, then down to a walk. The signals for each gait were very different from one another. Starlight certainly knew them all, but as with any young horse, and Starlight was only four, he sometimes resisted changing gaits. A well-trained horse had to learn to respond instantly. Carole hoped very much that one day she would be able to ride Starlight in shows—maybe even at the level of national competition—and for that, she was going to need a very well-trained horse.

She was so focused on what she was doing that she

didn't even see Stevie arrive. When she looked up, Stevie was leaning on the fence with her chin in her hands, watching everything her friends were doing.

"I love seeing you work with Starlight," Stevie said.

"All it takes is patience," Carole said.

"And skill," Stevie said. "You've got a lot of that. Fortunately, Starlight also seems to have brains, so sometimes he remembers the things you teach him."

"Repetition. That's the secret to training a horse," Carole said. "They learn something one day and then forget an awful lot of it by the next day. As long as you keep repeating the lesson again and again and again, eventually most of it stays in their memory banks."

"I wish it were the same way with people," Stevie said.

"That's just what Carole and I were talking about earlier," Lisa said, bringing Samson over. Actually, she followed the foal to where Stevie was. Samson was a very curious young horse, and he was eager to greet Stevie. Lisa knew she ought to be in charge when she had him on a lead line, but he seemed so glad to see her friend that she couldn't say no. His eagerness might have had something to do with the sugar lump Stevie was offering him.

"You'll spoil him," Lisa cautioned.

"No way," Stevie said. "Besides, if I do, Carole will just finish the training properly and get rid of all the spoiling *I* do."

"Thanks," Carole said. She rode over to where her friends were now standing and leaning forward, patting Starlight on the neck. He'd been working hard and deserved a break.

Stevie patted him, too, and then gave him a sugar lump as well. Then she patted Samson. The foal nuzzled her neck and tickled her. She loved it. She giggled. "What's neat about Samson is that even when you're working him and training him, he's still sweet. I wish that were the case with brothers."

Lisa and Carole looked at one another. This had a distinctly ominous sound.

"Did something happen?" Carole asked.

"No, but it's going to. I mean something is definitely up," Stevie said.

"What makes you think so?" Lisa asked.

"It's Chad," Stevie said. "He's apparently got a new girlfriend."

"What's so strange about that?" Carole asked. "The average life span of a romance for Chad is about four days, right? So it seems like it's time for a switch."

Stevie smiled. It was true. Chad was notably fickle in his relationships. "I guess you're right," she admitted. "His lacrosse stick actually looks like a bowl of leftover alphabet soup! Anyway, what's funny isn't that he's got a new girlfriend, but who it is. Stand back, girls. It's Veronica diAngelo."

"*Our* Veronica diAngelo?" Lisa asked.

93

"There's another one?" Carole asked.

"You know what I mean," said Lisa.

"Yeah, ours," Stevie said. "I saw them together at school today. They were giggling. The only time Chad ever giggles is with his girlfriends."

"Maybe it's just because he's been in love with every other girl at Fenton Hall and the only one left was Veronica," Lisa suggested.

Carole and Stevie looked at her. That was a thought with some merit in it.

"And the good news is," Lisa continued, "it will only go on for another four days."

"Unless he marries her," Carole chimed in, "in which case, the whole Lake family can retire on her money."

"I'd rather work, thank you very much," Stevie said.

"The thought of Veronica as a family member is enough to ruin anybody's day," Lisa said. "So I'm glad you came to us with your troubles. We know just how to help you get your mind off of them."

"What's that?" Stevie asked.

"Mucking out stalls," Carole said. "Mrs. Reg was here earlier and said that three of them needed cleaning."

"Where's the nearest pitchfork?" Stevie asked.

Mucking out stalls was not anybody's favorite job. If Stevie was eager to do it, her friends realized that she must really be worrying about her brothers. They were glad she had come to them. They would put her to work and get her mind off her troubles.

"Follow me," Lisa said.

"I don't need to. I can follow my nose," Stevie teased.

10

STEVIE BOUNCED OUT of bed before her alarm had finished sounding its first "ding." It was pitch-black outside, but that didn't matter. It would be light by seven o'clock, when the hunt would begin. Until then, there were a zillion things she had to do—if only she could remember any one of them. She rubbed her eyes and headed for the bathroom, pretty sure she would know what it was she was supposed to do by the time she finished brushing her teeth. It was hard to remember to be logical when every bit of her concentration was shattered by her excitement about the fox hunt that would start in— she squinted and tried to focus on the clock—two hours.

*　　*　　*

IT WASN'T HARD for Lisa to concentrate. Concentration was her specialty. However, she was already so organized that there wasn't much for her to concentrate on. On Friday night, she'd laid out everything she would need to put on in the morning, in the order that she'd put them on. Underwear, socks, jodhpurs, shirt, boots, jacket. Everything was there. She was out of bed, washed, and dressed in fifteen minutes. She loved her special hunting clothes—the snowy-white shirt with its white stock tie and the pin to hold the tie in place. The trim tweed jacket made her look so wonderfully formal. She smiled at herself in the mirror. Then all she had to do was to sit and wait for the clock to say six o'clock so she could leave for Pine Hollow. That was a mere forty-five minutes.

CAROLE WENT THROUGH her checklist a final time. She had to be sure to bring all of Starlight's tack in the van with her horse. She'd need his saddle and bridle, of course, and the saddle pad. Then she'd also need her own grooming bucket. It was a good thing she'd remembered to pack her extra saddle soap. Her saddle was actually pretty clean, but there was no telling if somebody else might need it. It was best to be prepared. She didn't want to disappoint her horse. Also, she had a new curry comb, and she wanted to take that. She dropped it into the bucket.

Then she thought about sugar lumps and carrots.

She didn't like to give Starlight too many treats, but there was going to be some rough riding today, and Starlight would deserve a special snack. He also might like an apple. She burrowed into the vegetable drawer and emerged with a bruised apple that her horse would love.

She stopped in the middle of the kitchen, trying to think if she'd forgotten anything. Yes. She had left her riding hat up in her room, and she had to make sure her father was ready to drive her to Pine Hollow. She dashed up the stairs, calling out to her dad as she ran into her room.

"I'll be right there," Colonel Hanson assured her. "I'll meet you in the car."

Carole snapped her hat on her head. It was the easiest way to carry it. Then she dashed down the stairs again, picked up her grooming bucket, went through the kitchen door into the garage, and climbed into the front seat of the car. She fastened her seat belt and waited patiently for her father.

In just a minute, the driver-side door opened and Colonel Hanson got in. He looked over at his daughter. A smile crossed his face.

"Haven't you forgotten something?" he asked gently.

Carole didn't think so. She thought she'd remembered everything Starlight could possibly need. Then she looked down. The first hint that something was wrong was when she saw she was still wearing her fuzzy pink slippers. Another look confirmed her worst suspicions. She was also still wearing her pink-flowered pajamas.

"Uh, I'll be just a minute," she said.

Twenty-five minutes later, Carole's father dropped her off at Willow Creek. She was fully dressed and ready to ride. She also had her father's sworn promise that he would never tell anybody what she'd done that morning. Carole knew her father wouldn't tell, but she also knew that even if he did, nobody would be surprised. It was just like Carole to remember everything in the world for her horse and nothing for herself. Carole didn't mind that about herself. Nobody else seemed to, either.

"Hi!" she said, greeting Stevie and Lisa, who had both arrived sooner. "You look wonderful in your hunt clothes!"

"You, too," Lisa said. Carole smiled to herself, wondering briefly what Lisa would have said if she'd actually arrived in her pajamas, fuzzy slippers, and riding hat.

"Did you see what I saw?" Stevie asked, changing the subject.

Lisa shrugged. "What was it?"

"Veronica diAngelo."

"No way," Carole said. "Even Veronica wouldn't have the poor judgment to try to get in on the hunt at the last minute—not after she was so officially disinvited a week ago. You think you saw her *here?*"

Stevie shook her head in confusion. "It's early and I could be all wrong, but I don't know another chauffeur-driven Mercedes-Benz in this part of the state, and I know I saw one. It was pulling onto the road a couple of miles from here, out of a big empty parking lot. It was heading back toward Willow Creek when I saw it."

"So, who cares?" Lisa asked. "Even if it was Veronica, the good news is that she was going away from here. She won't be here to ruin the hunt for us today, will she?"

"Sometimes people who don't get enough sleep do and see some very strange things," Carole said with authority. "I'm sure it was all in your imagination."

"I hope so," Stevie said. "Because I can't think of a good reason why Veronica would be anywhere near here, but I can think of a lot of bad ones."

"Oh, come on, stop being so paranoid," Lisa said.

"Paranoid? Who's paranoid?" Phil asked, joining the girls. "My friend Stevie?" He was teasing and Stevie knew it. She smiled when she saw him. "Maybe it's just because she's afraid that the real fox is going to give us a better hunt than she did."

"No way!" Stevie said. Her friends were pretty sure she was right about that.

A big truck pulled into the driveway then, and there was a terrible din from the back of it.

"Methinks the hounds have arrived!" Phil announced, and the girls and Phil walked over to where the truck had stopped.

Hounds, Stevie thought. There really were hounds, and there really was a fox somewhere out there. Suddenly the whole idea of a fox hunt was very real. It wasn't just something to look forward to. It was something she was doing! She felt a chill and got goose bumps. She, Stevie Lake, was about to go on a real fox hunt.

Stevie wanted to watch the owner unload his hounds, but it was time to unload their horses from the Pine Hollow vans and tack them up. The hunt began in just twenty minutes, and all the riders would be subject to an inspection before that. There wasn't a minute to waste.

Tacking up their own horses wasn't hard for The Saddle Club. They'd been doing that ever since their first days at Pine Hollow. Another thing they'd been doing since those first days was helping others, and that took longer. Once Topside had his tack on and Stevie was sure both she and her horse could withstand any inspection, she looked around to see who needed her help.

Nearby, May was having a little trouble with Luna. The pony didn't like riding on a van and seemed to be in a nasty mood. He wouldn't let May tighten the girth.

May was about to give up and climb into the saddle anyway.

"Uh-uh," Stevie said. "It's got to be good and tight whenever you ride, but particularly on a ride like a hunt. If a saddle is loose, it can just slip upside down, and that always happens at the worst possible time, like when you're going over a fence. If the saddle turns upside down, imagine what would happen to you!"

"Can you help me?" May asked.

"Don't I always?" Stevie said. "That's what friends are for. Besides, I'm stronger than you are."

Stevie suggested that May hold Luna's bridle and try to distract the pony with affection and pats while Stevie tended to the girth. She lifted up the skirt of the saddle and examined the buckle, estimating she'd want to move it two holes tighter. She listened to May chatter with the pony, and she watched the pony's belly. One thing horses and ponies often did when they wanted to keep somebody from tightening a girth too much was to take a big breath of air and try to fool the human being. Stevie was not about to be fooled by a pony. She watched the movement in the horse's chest and belly carefully. As soon as she saw him breathe out, she took hold of the leather and pulled. Three notches later, she was satisfied that the saddle was tight enough. Luna looked over his shoulder at

Stevie. She was sure she was getting a dirty look from the pony, but she was equally sure she hadn't hurt him and that she'd made him much safer for May to ride. She gave May a boost into the saddle and led her out to the area in front of the stable where all the riders were collecting.

"Look at all the dogs!" May said excitedly. She began to climb down out of the saddle so she could play with them.

"Hounds," Stevie said. "Remember? And they're working animals, not pets. Max said we wouldn't be allowed to pat them at all."

"Oh, right," May said, and she sounded very disappointed.

"I heard the trainer say something about how we could feed them their breakfast—after the hunt. Will that be okay?"

"It'll have to be, huh?"

Stevie smiled. May was eager to be in on everything and to do everything right. She was really a great kid, and Stevie liked doing things with her. She was sort of like a little sister that Stevie had never had, and that made her a whole lot better than all the brothers she did have.

Stevie told May she was going to fetch Topside and she should wait for her there. The two of them could start out together in the hunt. May seemed to think that was a good idea.

Stevie had to walk through the place where the hounds were being held in order to get to Topside. Max was there, talking with the hounds' owner, who seemed more than a little concerned about something. Although Stevie didn't always listen to everything that was said to her, she almost never missed the opportunity to eavesdrop on something other people were saying to one another.

"Why are they making so much noise?" Max asked.

"Fox must have been right through here," the owner said. "They've picked up a scent for sure, and they are ready to go. If they are this excited, the fox may be nearby. This may be a short hunt."

Stevie couldn't listen a whole lot longer without being too obvious about it, particularly after Max gave her a dirty look. She moved on and mounted Topside, hoping the hounds' owner was wrong. She was looking forward to a good long hunt and a lot of fun while they did it.

Soon all the riders were gathered and ready for inspection. While Max looked them over, Mr. Baker gave final instructions. He introduced the hounds' owner, a man named Chester, who would ride with them, and he introduced Chester to Lisa, the Junior Master, and Phil, the junior huntsman. Stevie was very excited for her friends and the honors they had, leading the hunt. There was a little twinge of envy this time that she didn't get to play a starring role as she had with the mock hunt, but it was okay and she knew it. This time, it was for real.

Chester stood in the middle of a circle of hounds, all on leashes that paired them together. "They're called couples," he reminded them. "Today, we have twelve and a half couples to hunt with. In case you need help with your math, that means twenty-five hounds." The young riders laughed. "And these guys are raring to go. Are you ready?"

The young hunters all nodded. They were as ready as they were going to be.

"Then let's be off."

At these words, Max, who always seemed to have a way of surprising his young riders, did it again. He pulled a short brass horn out of a bag, raised it to his lips, and blew a very rapid one-note call. The riders didn't know the name of it, but they all knew what it meant.

Chester released the hounds, and the hunt began.

11

"WHAT'S THE MATTER?" Stevie asked Chester when she saw the totally confused look on his face. The hunt had started just thirty seconds earlier, and already it seemed that something was amiss.

"It's the hounds," he said. "They should be following the scent, and Mr. Baker was sure it would head over to the east. Instead the hounds are running around in circles in the yard here, and they all look like they're going crazy."

That part was definitely true. Stevie and the other young riders had expected to take off with a bang, but it seemed that they were standing still with a bang—or at least with a howl—because that was the sound the hounds were making. They were dashing in and out among the legs of the horses, some of whom weren't very used to smaller creatures running around their legs, and some of whom were getting nervous about it. Stevie had already advised May to hold onto her reins very tightly. Luna was definitely jumpy. Topside was doing all right, but Starlight didn't like all the activity at all. Fortunately, Carole was in complete control.

Then one of the hounds put his nose to the ground, took a few tentative steps forward, and began a new kind of bark altogether.

"He's got something! It's a find!" Chester announced. Stevie remembered that meant the hound had found the trail. At the new bark, all the other hounds looked up. Obviously, in hound-talk, the word was out that they were ready to go—and go they did— right into the barn!

"No way was there a fox in here!" Mr. Baker said indignantly.

"Something was," Chester said, a little irritated with all the confusion.

However, since the hounds seemed so sure of themselves, there was nothing to do but to follow them. Lisa gave Diablo a little kick, and all the riders followed—right through the barn.

If a fox had been in the barn, it was clear that he didn't stay there for long. In an instant, the hounds were through the barn, followed by forty riders on horseback, and then they aimed straight for Mr. Baker's house!

Twenty-five hounds raced up onto the front portico. Forty horses and riders stopped short of going up the steps. Twenty-five hounds traipsed the full length of the portico and dashed around the rear of the house. Forty horses and riders followed, not on the portico, of course, just along the edge, through Mr. Baker's flower patch. Twenty-five hounds sped through the laundry yard under flapping white sheets. Forty horses and riders bolted right after them, unable to stop before running into the sheets. Five sets of very dirty sheets lay trampled in the muddy dirt of the laundry yard. Two laundry poles lay next to them.

"What's going on here!" Mrs. Baker called out angrily.

"Nothing, dear," Mr. Baker assured her. "It's just a little—oh, well, I'll help you later, okay?"

Nobody wanted to wait around to hear the answer to that. Nobody could, anyway. Before Mrs. Baker could gather her laundry and her wits for an appropriate retort, the hounds were off again—this time scurrying under the Baker children's swing set and then right through the pumpkin patch next to it. Forty horses and riders made a mess of the few pumpkins still ripening. Mr. Baker's face showed his distress. Chester's face showed only confusion.

"Something's definitely wrong," he said to Max. Max didn't have a chance to answer. The hounds were moving so fast, all any of the riders could do was follow them at breakneck speed.

Within seconds, twenty-five hounds and forty riders were on the road. The fox's scent stopped dead at the roadside. The whippers-in, whose job it was to keep the hounds fanned out until they could pick up the scent again, began milling around the pack.

Then there was a howl, the sound the riders had come to know as the sign that the hounds had found something. It was on the other side of the road. Twenty-five hounds and forty riders crossed the road. The trail followed the edge of the road for a hundred yards or so, taking all the hounds and all the riders right over a sewer pipe, and then it stopped dead again.

"Let's see if it picks up on the other side of the road," Stevie suggested. Sure enough, there it was.

"THIS IS WEIRD," Chester said. "The scent doesn't do this. The hounds don't act this way. This behavior is not normal for hounds following the line of a real fox. Smells don't leap across roads. Something's fishy."

Chester's use of the phrase "real fox" struck Stevie as odd. She wanted to ask him what he meant, but as a junior whipper-in, it seemed presumptuous to question Chester. Meanwhile, the combination of the strange behavior of the hounds, the weird trail of the scent, and the unexplained presence of the diAngelo's Mercedes so early that morning were making Stevie very suspicious, and very unhappy. She was building up the nerve to question Chester when the hounds started yowling again, and they were off.

The hunt continued in just that strange way for another half an hour. Even though Chester, Max, and Mr. Baker kept saying that this was all very strange, the young riders were having a great time. This was very different from their usual trail ride, and somehow having the adults so confused made it all the more fun. That is, everybody was having fun except Stevie. She was getting a very bad feeling about it all.

"The hounds have the scent again!" Chester announced. This time the hounds raced like crazy in a straight line—very different from what had been going on. Twenty-five hounds dashed right along the edge of the road, followed by forty riders. Then they took a sharp right turn, directly into the parking lot where Stevie had seen Veronica's Mercedes that morning. The only occupants parked there now were the trucks and trailers for the Emerson Circus. Stevie remembered that this was where the circus was going to perform in Cross County—unless, of course, twenty-five hounds led forty riders on a merry chase through the big top, wreaking as much damage there as they had in Mrs. Baker's laundry yard. The hounds seemed to have something else in mind, however. They dashed wildly up to a lamppost in the center of the lot, and they stopped, completely and totally.

"Are we to assume the fox climbed the lamppost?" Max asked, looking up. The tone of his voice indicated that the way Chester had trained his dogs left something to be desired.

"They just follow their noses, Mr. Regnery," Chester said unapologetically. "Their noses tell them something stopped here."

"If the fox went to ground here, we've got a new burrowing and digging tool that the construction industry is going to want to know about," Mr. Baker said. He wasn't thrilled with Chester's hounds, either.

Stevie watched and listened. Her stomach turned with every word.

"Boy this fox *is* cleverer than you were!" Lisa whispered to her. Carole laughed. Stevie didn't.

"It's not a fox," Stevie said, finally speaking her concern aloud.

"If it's not a fox, what is it?" Carole asked.

"It's my brothers, and Veronica," Stevie said. "I don't know what they've done, but it's something. This whole thing just smells of trouble, and I'm the cause of it."

"No way," said Lisa. "They promised."

Stevie looked at her sharply. "What do you mean, they promised?" she asked.

Carole gasped. Lisa realized what she'd done. She hadn't meant to say anything about Stevie's brothers. The words had just come out of her mouth before she'd even had a chance to finish thinking the thought, but maybe it wouldn't matter now if Stevie knew. She hoped it wouldn't anyway.

She gulped. "Carole and I were worried about them. We met them and asked them if they were plotting revenge."

Stevie stared at her friends. "You talked to my conniving brothers?"

"Yes, we did," Carole said. "We wanted to be sure they wouldn't do anything to ruin the fox hunt. They said that they weren't mad at you; you'd just been getting even with them. Lisa's right. They promised they wouldn't do anything. In fact, they were even interested to learn about the hunt. They asked us all kinds of questions."

Stevie loved her friends very dearly, and she never wanted anything to hurt their friendship, especially not her brothers. However much it bothered her that Lisa and Carole had gone behind her back to talk to her brothers, it was nothing compared with her astonishment that her friends would actually believe anything that threesome had said to them!

"And what did you tell them?" Stevie asked, realizing that she was at last getting to the bottom of this all.

"Everything," Lisa said. "We explained the differences between a mock hunt and a real hunt and a drag hunt—you know, that kind of thing."

Then it all came together for Stevie. The last thing in the world she wanted was to have to admit the whole thing to Max, but there was no way to put a pretty face on it. She'd blown the fox hunt for everybody in Horse Wise and Cross County just because of her silly feud with her brothers.

Reluctantly she rode over to where Max, Chester, and Mr. Baker were about to come to blows.

"I know what it is," she said. The three men stopped talking to one another and turned to Stevie. "It's all my fault, because my brothers and Veronica are angry with me, and this is their way of getting back." Then, as fast as she could do it, because she didn't want to prolong the agony, Stevie explained. She explained about how her brothers had learned about drag hunts, and that she'd seen Veronica there earlier that morning.

"I'm sure what she did was to take a bag of something that would draw the hounds and pull it behind her, probably on foot, but maybe with a bicycle. Can't you just see her laying the trail across Mr. Baker's porch and through the laundry yard?"

Max nodded sadly. "I guess I can," he said. "And I guess I owe you an apology," he said to Chester. "It's not your hounds after all."

"I knew there was something fishy about it all," Chester said. "These hounds will always follow a good line—unless something distracts them, like a fresh drag."

The look on Mr. Baker's face right then told Stevie she was about to be formally disinvited to the Cross County hunt. She knew she deserved it, but it made her very sad.

"Would you excuse us for a moment, Stevie?" Max asked. "We need to talk."

Sure they did. They had to talk about what kind of humiliation and punishment they were going to impose on Stevie. She turned Topside around and rode away from the other riders and the hounds who milled around the parking lot waiting for something to happen. This was a sad day for her.

While the three men conferred, Stevie watched the activities of the Emerson Circus, deciding she might as well get an eyeful now because there was no way her parents would take her or her brothers this year. Nor did they deserve to go.

That was sad, too. It was small consolation that she had a chance now to watch the elephants at work. Elephants were wonderful animals, so big, yet so graceful. A big old bull elephant was working to set up the tent. First he picked up a long pole and carried it to the center of the parking lot, where the circus's roustabouts set it upright. Then, using the elephant to tighten the lines, the roustabouts secured the pole well. The elephant then carried another pole for the workmen. It was really fun to watch, and Stevie thought she could have sat there all day until the wind shifted, and she got a noseful of the unpleasant part of the circus. Then she leaned forward and patted Topside on the neck. It was a good thing she liked to ride horses instead of elephants, she told the horse. "Imagine what it would be like to muck out an elephant's stall." Topside didn't seem to think that was funny. Stevie laughed all by herself.

"Uh, Stevie, would you come over here?" Max called her.

That brought Stevie back from her thoughts of elephants to the reality of the ugly situation she'd created. Now she was about to find out what her fate was.

"We've had a little talk," Max said. "We agree with you that this has come about because of your actions, and you know we have talked in the past about the problems with practical jokes." He glared at her. However, Stevie thought there was just the tiniest hint of a twinkle in the glare. What was going on? "One thing we know about you, Stevie, is that if there's a tricky problem, you are always more likely than anybody else to come up with a tricky solution. We'll give you a shot here. Can you think of a way to salvage this situation? To get the hounds back to Cross County and off the scent of the drag so that they can pick up the line of a fox? One chance to save yourself, Stevie. This is it."

One thing she could always say about Max was that he was fair. He was giving her an opportunity to make it up to the other riders. She didn't want to blow it. She looked around. Her friends were regarding her curiously. The hounds were still barking wildly. No help there. Then she looked at the elephant again, being led back to his holding pen now that all of the poles had been secured. That's when it came to her.

"What if we mask the scent of the drag with a stronger, more frightening and unpleasant smell?" Stevie asked.

Max, Chester, and Mr. Baker followed Stevie's eyes to the elephant.

Chester summed it up in one word.

"Ingenious," he said.

Mr. Baker's face lit up brightly. "Ah, yes!"

Max spoke to his colleagues. "Would you excuse us, please? Stevie and I have some fast-talking to do." Together Max and Stevie rode over to the elephant trainer.

Fifteen minutes later, the hunt was on again, only this time in reverse. And this time it was being led not by a huntsman and a Master, but by an elephant. The pachyderm, Jumbo by name, lumbered slowly and steadily along the edge of the road leading back to

Cross County, switching from side to side, erasing the scent of the drag with each step while it left its own pungent odor.

The Junior Master and huntsman were assigned to ride on either side of the elephant while it trod along the highway. Lisa and Phil found themselves talking to Jumbo's trainer, who sat on the elephant's back, right behind his ears.

"I wouldn't usually do this kind of thing, you know," the man said. "But that girl—what's her name? Johnny?—she was so convincing. I bet she could talk anybody into doing anything!" He'd gotten Stevie's name wrong, Lisa thought, but he sure had gotten her personality right!

12

AFTER COMPLETELY MASKING the drag trail, there was one more little job Jumbo took on for the hunt. He helped Mrs. Baker put the poles back up in her laundry yard.

Then Chester led twenty-five hounds and forty riders into a nearby field, far enough from the farm so that the hounds wouldn't be confused by the scent of the drag or of the elephant and into an area where they were, in fact, likely to pick up the scent of a fox.

This time everything was different. This time the hounds circled eagerly, not frantically. Chester watched proudly. He knew when things were going right. Soon enough, one of the hounds started barking loudly. Then all the others joined in.

"He's got the line!" Chester announced. They were off—for real!

Stevie, Carole, Lisa, and Phil all rode together, the Master, the huntsman, and two whippers-in had a good excuse to stay together. Right there, too, was May. She was more than game and didn't want to miss anything.

Lisa had been riding long enough to begin to be sort of matter-of-fact about it. She loved it, but it usually didn't have the thrill that she remembered from her first few experiences. Today it had that thrill. Diablo seemed to feel the excitement and urgency of the hunt. A few of the horses were a little skittish around the hounds, but not Diablo. It was as if he understood the important part the hounds were playing in the fun. No matter what else was going on with him, his eyes never seemed to leave the pack of hounds who scurried forward through the field. Diablo wanted to be right there, in the middle of it all.

At first the hounds moved cautiously forward, sniffing the ground for the fox's scent as they went. Then their heads rose, and they began running faster.

Lisa knew what that meant. It meant the scent of the fox was breast-high so that the hounds could smell it without putting their noses down. It also meant the scent was stronger, likely more recent. And finally, it meant that the horses were going to canter or gallop. She looked at her friends and saw that they understood what was about to happen. Then she looked over her shoulder at the other riders. Some of them weren't paying much attention to the pack of hounds and were just enjoying the ride. That was fine, up to a point. If most of the horses started cantering, all of them would soon enough, with or without their riders' permission. At the very least, the riders needed to know.

Lisa tried raising an arm. Nobody noticed. She tried waving. That didn't work, either. Then she tried calling out. There was no response. The trouble was that the riders were just having too much fun.

She was getting really concerned when Max came to her rescue. He pulled the horn out of his pocket and raised it to his lips. A few notes sounded, and everybody was looking at him.

"Prepare to canter!" he hollered.

And they did.

The hounds bolted then, racing across an open field and then down into a glen. The horses followed at an incredibly fast rate. Lisa tried to concentrate on the horse beneath her, carrying her across the field, but it was hard not to notice the thundering field of other horses that surrounded her. She glanced this way and that, trying to see everything at once, and then decided that the only thing she could possibly focus on was where she was going.

It was a good thing, too, because where she and everybody else was going was over a fence! The hounds scooted over, under, and around it, but the horses wouldn't have as many choices.

Lisa shortened Diablo's reins and shifted her own weight forward and up in the stirrups. Diablo didn't hesitate. He knew exactly what was expected of him, and Lisa knew how to tell him to do it. As they neared the fence, a low wooden divider, she rose in the saddle and leaned forward, giving Diablo as much rein as he would need. Keeping herself well balanced and her weight centered above his withers, she let the horse do what she had told him to do. His front legs rose up off the ground, and then she felt the powerful surge of his rear legs impelling them forward and upward. They lifted off—two beings working as a single unit—and seemed to float over the fence. Diablo's front legs struck the ground first, and then his rear ones followed, seeming to be cantering even before Lisa realized they had landed. It was as if the horse hadn't missed a beat of the gait. Lisa sighed with pleasure. She had never felt anything so wonderful in her life as jumping with Diablo. From that moment on, what she most wanted to do on her fox hunt was to jump. Fortunately for her, it appeared that the fox was cooperating. The hounds led the riders over six more jumps before temporarily losing the scent.

Lisa wasn't sorry for a little time to rest while the hounds figured out what had happened to their quarry.

She'd discovered that exhilaration could be exhausting.

"I can't believe how much fun this is," Carole said, drawing close to Lisa, Stevie, and Phil. "But I'm having a problem."

"What is it?" Stevie asked, concerned.

Carole took a deep breath. "Well," she said. "As you, my best friends, know, I've been unable to decide what I want to be when I grow up. I can't decide among being a veterinarian, a show rider, a breeder, or a trainer."

"So?"

"Now I have to add fox hunter to the list," Carole said. "That's going to make it even tougher to decide!"

"Poor girl!" Stevie teased. "What a decision you're going to have to make *in ten years!*"

"So, in the meantime, you're going to have to spend all your spare time trying each of them—over and over again," Phil suggested.

"Isn't that just terrible?" Carole said, trying to hide her smile.

Stevie clapped her on the back. "It's a tough job, but somebody's got to do it," she said.

"For my part, I think I've made a decision," Lisa said. Her friends looked at her. "I want to jump horses—specifically Diablo."

"Oh, I forgot to mention that when I recommended

him to you, didn't I?" Carole asked. "He is a wonderful jumper, so he's perfect for fox hunting."

"It's like flying."

"That's the way good jumping should be," Carole said. She patted Starlight's neck as she spoke. Carole thought Starlight was a great jumper, certainly a very strong one, if not quite as smooth as Diablo. She didn't want her horse to have hurt feelings.

"Don't worry," Stevie said, seeing what she was doing. "He may appear to be nearly human sometimes, but I don't think he can understand what we're saying." Starlight lifted his head and seemed to give Stevie a dirty look as if she'd just insulted him.

Lisa and Phil laughed. So did Carole. Stevie wondered briefly if Carole had given Starlight a signal with the reins that made the horse look at her, but it didn't really matter. It had been funny, and she didn't mind being teased a little. She pretended to sulk and looked away from her friends.

It was a good thing she did because just at that moment, she spotted some motion in the grass about a quarter of a mile across the field. She squinted and shaded her eyes, wondering if the bright sunshine was playing tricks with her vision.

It wasn't. There was more movement and then the unmistakable look of a long furry tail.

She was so excited she could barely talk. "It's a . . . a . . . Did you see . . . ? Over there . . ." She pointed.

"Strange to see Stevie speechless," Phil remarked. "Usually we can't stop her from talking."

"Even when she shouldn't!"

"Look. . . . It's a . . ."

"There she goes again," Lisa joked.

Stevie's talking wasn't doing her any good, but her frantic pointing finally got somebody's attention.

"The fox! Stevie spotted the fox!" May shouted, waving wildly at Mr. Baker and Chester, who were closest to the animal.

"Master! Huntsman! Whippers-in!" Mr. Baker called. "We have to get the hounds on the line again!"

It took some organizing, but in a very short time, the whippers-in and the huntsman managed to head the hounds in the direction where Stevie and May had seen the fox. As soon as the hounds were turned around, one of them picked up the scent and began giving tongue. That was what hunters called the excited howl of a hound who knew he was hot on the trail of a fox. What one hound began, twenty-four others quickly picked up. The din was incredible; the excitement was so strong, it could be felt in the air.

Stevie thought it was only a matter of seconds before all the hounds and the riders were chasing across the field, pursuing the fox.

If what had happened before was fun—and it was— this was an incredible experience. Stevie could feel her own heart pounding with the excitement—or was it the beat of Topside's hooves thundering across the field after the fox? It didn't matter. The fact was, the whole experience was nothing short of thrilling.

The hounds led the riders across the field, into the woods, and through a glen, over fallen trees, around rocks, across creeks, and under branches. With each step, the hounds howled more loudly, each pushing to get to the front of the pack and be the first, panting and barking, eager to find their prey.

In turn the horses that followed the hounds seemed to feel the same way. The riders did whatever they had to in order to stay on and have the ride of their lives.

Starlight glided along the hillside, moving smoothly and speedily. Carole ducked beneath some branches and swept others aside. When Starlight prepared to jump, she followed along, for once letting her horse do the thinking. Everything was happening too fast for her to have time for thought. Her mind was processing all the experiences it could handle without taking charge. She found herself breathing hard, not because she was tired or worn out, but because she was simply excited. It was wonderful, beyond comparison to anything she'd ever done on horseback before.

And then it stopped, as quickly as it had started. The hounds were suddenly silent. They sniffed eagerly, but went nowhere, merely circling in a large open area surrounded by thick brush. The riders all drew to a halt, watching the hounds work, not wanting to interrupt them. They seemed to know how to do their job very well, as long as they weren't chasing a phony trail or an elephant.

"He's gone to ground," Lisa said.

A few riders nodded. They'd learned their fox hunting terminology. That meant that the fox had found a place to hide underground. When foxes did that, they were usually safe and the hunt was over.

"We'll wait awhile," Chester said. "Sometimes foxes make mistakes."

They waited. After twenty minutes, it was clear that the fox had simply outfoxed them all.

"Maybe the fox has gone back to Cross County for the hunt breakfast," Lisa suggested. "Certain other foxes have been known to do that kind of thing before."

Chester looked confused. Everybody else laughed. Max explained the joke to Chester. He smiled, too. Then Mr. Baker looked at his watch. It was almost noon, and it was going to take the riders another half an hour to get back to Cross County. It seemed like a good idea to call it a day and return to the stable. Although a few of the riders thought they would be more than willing to hunt the fox for the rest of their lives, the horses and the hounds seemed to be ready for a rest.

Max pulled out his horn and blew another call. The hunt was over. It was time to go home.

13

"SO, STEVIE AND Phil, tell me," Chad said very casually. "How was the fox hunt today? Anything interesting happen?"

What a question, Stevie thought. As if Chad didn't know the answer to it. Fortunately, however, she and Phil had discussed the issue on the way back to her house from Pine Hollow just an hour or so earlier. It was sure to come up, especially since Phil was having dinner with the Lakes again. Stevie did not want a repeat of the dinner two weeks earlier. Nor did she want to give her brothers one ounce of satisfaction.

"Oh, it was great," Phil said. "We went all over the woods by Cross County. Stevie even spotted the fox once."

"A real fox?" Alex asked. "Are you sure?"

"I definitely saw his tail," Stevie said. "And the hounds followed him all over the place. It was something."

"It was great," Phil added. "You can't imagine the adventure fox hunting is."

"Hmmm," Alex said.

"I don't get it," Michael said.

"I've never had a ride like that," Stevie said.

Chad glanced at his brothers, and an odd look crossed his face. Stevie stifled her smirk and was glad to see that Phil was doing the same. It was definitely working. They were driving her brothers crazy.

"Well, did you catch the fox?" Chad asked.

"No, of course not," Stevie said. "We never wanted to do that in the first place. I told you that. It's not about catching foxes. It's really just a fun kind of riding."

"The *most* fun," Phil added.

"But didn't anything unusual happen?" Alex asked.

"Ahem," Mrs. Lake said. She didn't know what was going on, but she clearly knew that something was going on, and she thought it was about time for her sons to stop pestering their sister and her friend.

"Yeah, like, did you spend a lot of time on the road?" Michael asked.

"Road? What road?" Stevie said.

Mr. Lake smelled a rat. "Boys, what's going on here?" he asked.

"Nothing," all three answered as a chorus.

Stevie smiled sweetly, innocently, pleased to find that she had convinced her brothers that that was exactly what had gone on.

After dinner Stevie said she thought it would be a good idea if she and Phil did the dishes. Mrs. Lake was more than a little surprised since Stevie was quite famous for doing everything in the world to get out of cleaning up after dinner.

"That's not necessary," she said. "You and Phil have had a long day. Why don't you just relax while your brothers do the dishes?"

That was precisely what Stevie had in mind. "Reverse psychology," she explained to Phil as the two of them escaped to the den in the basement. "We just had to get somewhere where we could laugh without their hearing us. You were perfect. Thank you."

The two of them sat on the comfortable old sofa in the den. Phil took Stevie's hand. "They're going to find out eventually," he said.

"Of course they are," she said. "Some of the other riders will certainly let them know, but for now the joke's on them, and that's all I really wanted."

"And your parents are going to find out, too. That means they'll find out everything, won't they?"

Stevie nodded. "They're going to be pretty angry about it, I know. We'll probably all get grounded, and if I know Dad, he's going to make good on his promise not to take us to the circus this year. I'll be sorry about that, but other than that, the whole thing has turned out wonderfully. The circus will be back in town next year. I can wait until then."

There was a sparkle in Phil's eyes that Stevie had come to know meant something good was on his mind.

"What is it?" she asked. "Why are you smiling like that?"

"Like what?"

"It's your dimple smile that makes you look like the cat that ate the canary."

"Not a canary, exactly," he said. His dimples deepened. He reached into his pocket. "More like an elephant," he said.

Stevie loved secrets when *she* was the one keeping them. She hated them when she had trouble prying them out of other people. She really wanted to know what Phil was up to.

"What are you doing?" she demanded.

"I just wanted to see if I had anything interesting in my pocket here." He pulled something out. "Oh, what's this?" he asked, trying to sound surprised. "Oh, my, my."

"Tickets?" Stevie said. Her mind raced. It could only be one thing. "To the circus?"

Phil nodded.

"How did you manage that?" she asked.

He shrugged modestly. "Jumbo's trainer seemed to

132

think that being on a fox hunt was the most fun thing
he'd done all day. He was looking for a way to thank
you for letting him join in. I just made a suggestion,
that's all. Are you free next Friday night?"

"You bet I am!" she said, grinning from ear to ear.
And then she thanked him with a kiss.

14

THE NEXT DAY, Stevie, Carole, and Lisa met at Pine Hollow for a Saddle Club meeting. It was bright, sunny, and cool in the paddocks. Lisa suggested that the meeting would be nice if they had it outdoors. Carole said that was true, and that it would be even better if they had it on horseback. Carole agreed with both of them, but suggested it would be best of all if they pretended they were still on the fox hunt.

One of the great things about sharing a love of horses with friends was that they just about never had any disagreement over what would be fun.

They got Max's permission to take a trail ride and tacked up their horses.

Lisa blew an imaginary horn to start the hunt. Carole saw to it that the hounds had a good head, meaning that they were fanned out appropriately to be able to pick up the line. Stevie stood up in her stirrups and shaded her eyes from the bright sun, looking for the fox.

The girls were enjoying themselves immensely. Pretend was *almost* as good as the real thing.

"I know I'll spot him in a minute," Stevie promised her friends. "These things just have a way of working out for me."

"Uh, we wanted to talk to you about that," Lisa said. She and Carole had spent half an hour on the phone the night before discussing Stevie's antics and the trouble they had caused. Both of them had agreed that they had to say something to Stevie about it. "Even though we all had a good time yesterday," Lisa continued, "and the hunt turned out all right, it was almost a disaster."

"How's that?" Stevie asked. She clicked her tongue and flicked her reins a little. Topside began walking easily toward the woods. Carole and Lisa signaled their horses to walk as well. It seemed more like a good time for a real walk than a pretend fox hunt.

"We were worried," Carole explained. "When you got into that silly feud with your brothers—"

"Was it silly? They were really horrible to me," Stevie said.

"Sure they were," Lisa agreed. "And then you were even more horrible to them, and then they were even *more* horrible to you, and then Veronica got into it, and she was trying to be the most horrible of all. Where does this all lead to?"

"It's all your practical joking," Carole added. "We just think it gets out of hand. You should consider giving up practical jokes and just live a normal life."

"Normal?" Stevie said, sounding as if she'd never heard the word. Then she shook her head. "I don't think so. I mean, look at what I've done for you. First of all, if I weren't the clever, devious kind of person I am, I never would have been a fox, much less a good fox, at the mock hunt, and if I hadn't been the fox, Veronica never would have been so excited about catching up with me that she would have crossed Mr. Andrews's land. So, point number one is that because of *me*, Veronica was thrown out of the hunts."

That was true. Lisa thought the argument was more than a little convoluted, but it was true. She conceded that Stevie had a point.

"And if that hadn't happened, Veronica never would have run into Chad, and the two of them never would have plotted with Alex and Michael to try to ruin the junior hunt."

"That's what we mean," Carole said. "See, all these ifs lead to trouble."

"Trouble?" Once again, the word sounded unfamiliar coming from Stevie. "That's not what I meant. When the four of them got the idea of making a drag trail, that turned a really great fox hunt into an outstanding fox hunt. I mean, if it weren't for me, you never would have had a chance to take an elephant on a fox hunt. You guys ought to be thanking me instead of trying to get me to change my ways." She grinned proudly. Her friends understood that she was smiling then because she was happy at the way she'd been able to turn their arguments inside out and make herself come out on top. She wasn't done, either.

"And, speaking of thanking me, you're about to do it again, because my sharp eye has just spotted a wily fox skirting the edge of the ravine over to the left. He's about to run through the creek, dash along the top of the fallen tree by the big old rock, and then scootch under the pile of brush next to the alfalfa field. The hounds, as you can see, are positively going wild. I think that if we hurry—really hurry—we can catch up with him by the time he reaches the fallen tree. Tally-ho!"

She was off.

Carole and Lisa looked at one another, stunned. They'd never known anyone quite like Stevie before, and they were sure they wouldn't ever again. She could be strange, wild, and definitely incorrigible, but she could also be an awful lot of fun. Maybe it wasn't such a bad combination after all.

"Arf, arf!" Carole howled.

"After the hounds!" Lisa agreed.

ABOUT THE AUTHOR

BONNIE BRYANT is the author of more than fifty books for young readers, including novelizations of movie hits such as *Teenage Mutant Ninja Turtles* and *Honey, I Shrunk the Kids*, written under her married name, B. B. Hiller.

Ms. Bryant began writing The Saddle Club in 1986. Although she had done some riding before that, she intensified her studies then and found herself learning right along with her characters Stevie, Carole, and Lisa. She claims that they are all much better riders than she is.

Ms. Bryant was born and raised in New York City. She lives in Greenwich Village with her two sons.

THE SADDLE CLUB

A blue-ribbon series by Bonnie Bryant

Stevie, Carole and Lisa are all very different, but they *love*
horses! The three girls are best friends at Pine Hollow
Stables, where they ride and care for all kinds of horses.
Come to Pine Hollow and get ready for all the fun and
adventure that comes with being 13!